A Library of Modern Religious Thought

DAVID HUME

The Natural History of Religion

A LIBRARY OF
MODERN RELIGIOUS THOUGHT
General Editor: Henry Chadwick, D.D.

S. T. COLERIDGE
CONFESSIONS OF AN INQUIRING SPIRIT
Edited by H. StJ. Hart

LESSING'S THEOLOGICAL WRITINGS
Selected and translated by Henry Chadwick

DAVID HUME
THE NATURAL HISTORY OF RELIGION
Edited by H. E. Root

S. KIERKEGAARD
JOHANNES CLIMACUS and A SERMON
Translated and edited by T. H. Croxall

JOHN LOCKE
THE REASONABLENESS OF CHRISTIANITY
Edited and abridged by I. T. Ramsey

THE MIND OF
THE OXFORD MOVEMENT
Edited by Owen Chadwick

DAVID HUME

THE NATURAL HISTORY OF RELIGION

EDITED WITH AN INTRODUCTION

BY

H. E. ROOT, M.A.

FELLOW OF EMMANUEL COLLEGE, CAMBRIDGE

STANFORD UNIVERSITY PRESS

STANFORD, CALIFORNIA

Stanford University Press
Stanford, California
Copyright 1956 A. and C. Black Ltd.
Original American Edition 1957
Printed in the United States of America
ISBN 0-8047-0333-7
Last figure below indicates year of this printing:
81   80   79   78

CONTENTS

NOTE ON THE TEXT

The text followed in this edition is that established by T. H. Green and T. H. Grose and printed in their critical edition of Hume's *Essays, Moral, Political, and Literary* (London: Longmans, 1875). It is substantially the same as Hume's own definitive edition published in 1777 shortly after his death. Green and Grose's textual footnotes have been omitted in this edition. Those which remain, with all their oddities, are Hume's. In many places, however, the references to classical authors have been corrected or extended by Green and Grose; and in one or two places this edition corrects minor errors in their references.

The story of the publication of *The Natural History of Religion*, the suppression of the intended first edition of 1756 and the circumstances surrounding the early editions, is a remarkable one. Green and Grose give the facts as far as they knew them in their "History of the Editions" (*The Philosophical Works of David Hume*, Vol. III, pp. 60 ff.). A recent and fascinating account of the story is given by E. C. Mossner in his article "Hume's *Four Dissertations*: An Essay in Biography and Bibliography" (*Modern Philology*, xlviii (1950), pp. 37–57).

EDITOR'S INTRODUCTION

The Natural History of Religion first appeared nearly two hundred years ago in 1757, but despite this venerability its historical significance is not always realized. It could well be claimed that Hume's two complementary works, *The Natural History of Religion* and the *Dialogues Concerning Natural Religion*, mark the beginning of what is now generally, if loosely referred to as the philosophy of religion. Religion and religious beliefs had, of course, more ancient students, but as a study pursued systematically, critically and as a distinct part of philosophy it has little considerable history before Hume. If *The Natural History of Religion* is regarded as a specimen of the comparative study of religion, a precursor might be found in Lord Herbert of Cherbury's *De Religione Gentilium,* published in 1663. Hume's method and intent, however, are so widely different from Herbert's that a search for the influence of the earlier upon the later is not likely to be very profitable. Herbert began with the conviction that there was a kind of highest common factor of religious beliefs. This was the original religion of mankind, based upon belief in a Supreme Deity and rational and moral throughout. When Herbert turned to look at actual religions he could only conclude that their beliefs and practices were dreadful corruptions and distortions of that pure and undefiled prototype. Like Hume he found no lack of evidence for saying that religion as practised was both irrational and corrupt, but he did not abandon his notion of the original nature of religion and the idea passed into that stock of ideas about religion held later by the Deists. Hume, as one might expect from a thoroughgoing empiricist, saw even more clearly the corruption and irrationality. But it was precisely these features which led him to believe that a crude polytheism (at times he preferred to call it Idolatry) was verily the original religion of mankind. Theism (or monotheism) developed from it only hesitantly and with frequent set-backs. On this reading of the history of religion one cherished conviction of the Deists fell to the ground, and there is nothing to make us think that Hume regretted this consequence.

Hume's interpretation of such data as he had (and it was very limited, sometimes misleading and sometimes false) anticipated by many years the sort of story about the origin and development of religion which most anthropologists and many psychologists have told in our own time. But as the evidence accumulates, both about ancient man and about contemporary primitive men, the story becomes more rather than less complex. It is probably doubtful that Hume's certainties about religious development can now be thought obvious conclusions from our present state of knowledge. There is at least some evidence that among certain peoples a monotheistic belief, however impure or attenuated, may have been earlier than polytheism; and this primitive monotheism may have been grounded upon a more reflective view of the world and life than Hume would have been happy to admit. The idea that beliefs, and especially religious beliefs, develop in time in a perfectly orderly and straightforward way from the less to the more civilized has a great hold upon our minds, however much the evidence may be against it. Hume was not exempt from this desire to find an orderly pattern, even though he did allow that there was a certain "flux and re-flux" of theism and polytheism. But the accuracy of Hume's guesses and inferences is really a matter of little interest. Much more important is his view of the general character of religion and the method he uses to bring out this character. Our knowledge of the facts of religious development has grown enormously in the last two hundred years. It is not self-evident, however, that Hume's judgements about the general character of religion (or, for that matter, our own judgements) are wholly based upon such factual knowledge. Part of the significance of *The Natural History of Religion* is that upon analysis it so often shows how and why this is so.

A modern reprint of *The Natural History of Religion* is undoubtedly an acknowledgment of its importance, but at the same time some may think it odd to find it classed as a text illustrative of modern theology. The professedly religious and theological thinkers of Hume's day found it nothing but subversive and dangerous. Thus the famous Warburton felt compelled to write to Hume's publisher, Andrew Millar, that its purpose was "to establish *naturalism*, a species of atheism, instead of religion." To the greater part of the mid-eighteenth century religious public it was at best too sceptical and at worst an outrage. Similar feelings might still be aroused in spite of our more lenient view of what should and what should not be said about religion. Theologians may now be less eager than were Warburton and Hurd to rush into print in condemning dangerous books, but the religious man is no less sure that he can recognize an anti-religious book when he sees one. He may find it hard to understand why he ought to recognize it as an illustration of modern theology.

Hume did not parade an anti-religious attitude in the fashion of a writer for the Rationalist Press Association. In the very first paragraph of *The Natural History of Religion* he says, "The whole frame of nature bespeaks an Intelligent Author; and no rational inquirer can, after serious reflection, suspend his belief a moment with regard to the primary principles of genuine Theism and Religion." But against this near-profession of belief (it is not without ambiguity) we shall have to balance the criticism to which Hume subjects it in the *Dialogues Concerning Natural Religion*. Whatever our desires in the matter we shall find it hard to avoid Professor Norman Kemp Smith's judgement that the positive content of Hume's belief was, at the very most, severely restricted. Whether Hume retained genuine respect for "the primary principles of genuine Theism and Religion," or whether he was merely willing, at times, to work within the conventions of his age are questions largely of biographical interest. What we are left with is the argument itself and the uncontestable fact of its subsequent influence, in various directions, upon religious thought. We may be at a safe enough distance not to be caught up with the frenzy of Hume's eighteenth century opponents, but there is no distance great enough to keep us safe from whatever is revealing or consequential in his argument. It is worth taking pains with *The Natural History of Religion* because in it we see a virtuoso display by a major philosopher in the interpretation of religion. Such an interpretation is valuable in itself however we appraise its conclusions. But beyond that it may, if only by implication, help us to clarify our minds about the pressing and intricate question of the relation of philosophy to religion.

The most obvious, though not for that reason the simplest question one wants to ask about *The Natural History of Religion* is, What precisely was Hume trying to do? There is the beginning of an answer in its very first sentence: "As every enquiry, which regards religion is of the utmost importance, there are two questions in particular which challenge our attention, to wit, that concerning its foundation in reason, and that concerning its origin in human nature." The first of these questions is the subject of the *Dialog ;es Concerning Natural Religion*, and Hume turns his attention to the second in *The Natural History of Religion*. The implications of this division are not without interest. It seems perfectly legitimate to say that there are two sorts of questions which one can ask about any kind of belief: how it arose (its "cause"), and what the reasons are for believing it (its "truth"). For example we sometimes ask questions like these about the moral code and conventions of a particular people or group. With anthropologists (and perhaps psychologists) we may try to determine the causes and origins of moral notions. Or with philosophers and theologians we may ask how such notions are to be justified or whether they have any "foundation in reason." We should like to think that the first of these two sorts of questions is of the purely "scientific" kind, that there could be no ultimate disagreement about any real answers to them. Once we had assembled all the facts, all the relevant facts, the answers would be straightforward and indisputable. (As Hume wrote in another connection, ". . . after every circumstance, every relation is known, the understanding has no further room to operate . . ."). Furthermore we are inclined to suppose that to know the original occasion or cause or motive (observed or inferred) of a particular belief is to know the "real" reason why it is held. Therefore, we conclude, to determine the origin of religious beliefs and practices will be to answer questions as to why people entertain religious beliefs and indulge in religious practices.

One obvious danger about this tendency of thought is that questions about the truth of beliefs, their foundation in reason, come to seem superfluous once we think we know the reasons why they came to be held in the first place. We have become highly suspicious of the reasons men give when asked why they believe this or that, a suspicion which is manifested in our frequent description of such reasons as mere rationalizations. While we are glad to think that accounts of causes and origins are scientific, we are not so glad that discussions of truth and reasonableness are merely philosophical. For philosophical conclusions are things we can take or leave, but scientific ones have to be accepted lest we be thought foolish. In a scientific matter, we say, there can be only one correct answer; but disagreements about the reasonableness or appropriateness of beliefs seem unresolvable even when every circumstance, every relation is known. Of course argument and discussion can help to reveal whether our reasons are good or bad, cogent or fallacious. But we should much prefer to stay with the allegedly scientific answers and to suppose that they tell us all we need to know about religion. It is interesting that Hume cast his philosophical enquiry into dialogue form, a form in which disagreements could be clearly displayed. His enquiry into the origins and causes of religious beliefs is in the form of straight exposition. None the less it may well be that our inclinations are wrong, that conclusions about origins can be very philosophical, and that judgements about truth are not so unscientific. Although Hume saw fit to deal in two separate works with these two sorts of questions about religion, it is hard not to feel that the conclusions and implications of *The Natural History of Religion* make the *Dialogues* look like no more than exercises in illustration of the ingenuity of the human mind.

One of the major themes of *The Natural History of Religion* is Hume's firm conviction that there is always a wide gulf between any alleged rational basis for religion and the actual origins of religion in human nature and in history. In more than one place, as has been noted, he does seem to admit the cogency of a design argument for the existence of "invisible intelligent power." (This was the type of argument most cherished by his eighteenth century contemporaries, and its analysis was the chief business of the *Dialogues*.) But Hume was confident that such a reflective argument played no part whatever in the birth of such religion as is generally found among men. Man did not first believe because he beheld with wonder the remarkable order and regularity of nature. "On the contrary, the more regular and uniform, that is, the more perfect nature appears, the more is he familiarized to it, and the less inclined to scrutinize and examine it." "The first ideas of religion arose not from a contemplation of the work of nature, but from a concern with regard to the events of life, and from the incessant hopes and fears which actuate the human mind." To bring out the truth of this view of the real sources of religion he tells this story: "We hang in perpetual suspense between life and death, health and sickness, plenty and want; which are distributed amongst the human species by secret and unknown causes, whose operation is oft unexpected, and always unaccountable. These *unknown causes*, then, become the constant object of our hope and fear; and while the passions are kept in perpetual alarm by an anxious expectation of the events, the imagination is equally employed in forming ideas of those powers, on which we have so entire a dependence."

Hope and fear, unknown causes, imagination: these are the central features in Hume's account of religious origins. They are also a support for his view that polytheisms must be more primitive than theisms, for the "powers" are many and men naturally deal with them separately if they can. The power behind the good harvest can hardly be the one behind the untimely death of our first born. It may be, however, that all this is not so far from the elegant design argument of the Deists as Hume thought. The fact that men wish to hypostatize these unknown causes, real or imaginary, could be taken as evidence for a deep human conviction in the ultimate orderliness and explicability of things. It is like a more sophisticated teleology in that it does insist upon the existence of causes and rules out the possibility of pure chance. Hume did not draw this comparison, nor, when dealing with religion, was he anxious to suppose that there might be a kind of reasonableness even in human hopes, fears and imaginings.

Hume's conclusion about the true sources of religion is perhaps the central theory expounded in The Natural History of Religion, but there are important and interesting subsidiary ones. Sections IX-XIII are given up to a comparison of some of the effects of polytheism and monotheism. On all counts except that of "rationality" (and with qualifications even here) polytheism tends to come off better. It is not fanatically single-minded and is therefore less inclined to persecute; it fosters manly courage rather than shrinking abasement; and unencumbered by theological ideas or philosophical subtleties, it is more likely to be honest and straightforward. This final point assumes considerable importance in Hume's mind. He maintains that no matter how reasonable the foundation of theism, it will in practice still be full of superstitions and absurdities. If a philosopher is led to support theism because he sees point in postulating a Supreme Being, he cannot but end in nonsense and hypocrisy. "Where theism forms the fundamental principle of any popular religion, that tenet is so conformable to sound reason, that philosophy is apt to incòrporate itself with such a system of theology . . . But . . . philosophy will soon find herself unequally yoked with her new associate; and instead of regulating each principle, as they advance together, she is at every turn perverted to serve the purposes of superstition. For besides the unavoidable incoherences, which must be reconciled and adjusted, one may safely affirm, that all popular theology, especially the scholastic, has a kind of appetite for absurdity and contradiction."

None the less, if the philosopher must not serve neither can he ignore theology. He can examine and enquire and his enquiry assumes an almost prophetic role. This is not the sort of prophecy which is likely to prove popular, in any age, with the followers of what Hume called popular religion. Yet when we seek to understand what Hume was trying to do in *The Natural History of Religion* we may incorrectly suppose that his whole purpose was merely to debunk. This would be as serious a misunderstanding as to believe that the work was written just to give a Hume a chance to play a hand in the deistic controversies. That he does debunk is undeniable, but one does not bother to debunk unless one thinks one knows the real truth. We cannot doubt that Hume thought he knew the real truth about religion.

If we take it that *The Natural History of Religion* means to present us with an account of the real nature or essence of religion (as particularly revealed by the facts of religious origins), we want to know just what Hume understood religion to be. This sort of question may sound either incredibly simple or unnecessarily sly. As a rule we do not ask about the true nature of this or that thing (a table, a pencil, a typewriter). But should we be asked we would know more or less what to do. To one unfamiliar with typewriters we could describe their appearance and explain their use. Best of all, if we had one at hand, we could illustrate our talk with a performance. On the whole this kind of thing will satisfy the man (unless he is a philosopher) who asks about the nature of typewriters.

It is another matter when someone asks about the true nature of Matter or Mind or Love, or even Religion. Here we are apt to become nervous and hesitant, or else we turn back to our newspaper. We think such questions either a bit suspicious or else very abstruse and philosophical, and therefore not to be answered by ordinary men. For our own purposes we get along reasonably well when, for one reason or another, we find ourselves talking about the minds or the loves or the religions of people we know. But abstract discussion of such things (it usually begins when someone says, "But what do you mean by . . .?") gets tiresome and seems to lead nowhere. We know that philosophers have argued about these questions for centuries, without agreeing, and this is somehow intimidating. There is something wrong about this feeling of intimidation. It is obvious that the sorts of things we say in order to explain the nature of a typewriter have not the same character as the things we may want to say about the nature of religion. Disagreements about the nature of a typewriter are unlikely and would probably be foolish, but disagreements about the nature of religion are frequent and are certainly not foolish. It is a great virtue of *The Natural History of Religion* that it is not intimidating in the way that a discussion of the nature of religion might be. None the less it is a discussion of the nature of religion and not just a series of descriptions of religious beliefs and practices. The descriptions are so placed and so presented that in the end they add up to a definite theory and judgement of religion. To ask what Hume understood the nature of religion to be is not to ask whether he gives any abstract definitions of the Essence of Religion. It is more to ask what sort of descriptions and what sort of facts he thinks bring out the character of religion. For one thing we want to know whether *The Natural History of Religion* shows any signs that Hume thought religion, though complicated and perplexing, could be something more than just tiresome. To find this out we have to notice not only what he emphasizes but also what he leaves out.

Hume did not believe that religion was a "primary" constituent of human nature. He thought that there were men and nations in whom it was wholly absent, and for this reason he could not accord it so basic a role as the instincts of self-preservation and sex, or the dispositions of gratitude and resentment. He supposed that the principles (or causes) which first led to the development of religions were secondary in human nature and could therefore be brought to light and thoroughly understood by empirical study. This is probably the crucial assumption of his study. If you want to know what religion is, what it *really* is, then simply look at religious people and see what they profess and practise. Hume does not appear to have ever doubted that this was the best, or even the only way of going about the matter. In the working out of the method there is another idea which plays a prominent part. Religion *is* religious beliefs plus religious practices, but it is also a factor in human life and in the complex structure of human societies. It has, that is, certain definite and observable effects upon individuals and groups, effects which are particularly conspicuous in morals and politics. When drawing up a natural history one must look for these effects, and they will bulk large in a final account of what religion ultimately is. (This is not utterly unlike saying that an account of what a particular chemical substance is might well be made more concrete by mentioning that a very small amount of it will kill a horse.) Like the religious man who lays much stress on the saying, By their fruits ye shall know them, Hume thought it perfectly reasonable to suppose that the moral effects of religion are an important property of religion itself. This idea is of the greatest importance because it inevitably involves Hume in an implicit interpretation and evaluation of the facts he describes and therefore makes *The Natural History of Religion* a good deal more than just a natural history. Hume felt that any reasonable and educated man would be able, on the basis of the facts presented, to judge whether religion on the whole was a good or a bad thing. The moral and other effects of religion constitute, in a sense, its "cash value," and its "cash value" is its real value.

The plan of *The Natural History of Religion* is then to set before us a story about how religion began, to describe what (some) religious people believe and practise, and to give an account of how such belief and practice influence other sorts of opinion and behaviour. The vantage point of the writer is that of a detached outsider, recording what he sees and what he makes of it. He may at times be disdainful or nearly angry, but he is still outside and removed. He leaves us to draw our own final conclusions about the facts and in places shuns making explicit, in the form of a judgement, what is implicit in the facts which he brings to our attention. One might have expected him to say that if his theory of religious origins is correct, if religion is essentially the product of human unreason, then it is a subject scarcely worth the time of the enlightened man. In fact he never does this and can certainly not be found guilty of the so-called Genetic Fallacy. To make his point he has to go beyond the simple story of religious origins and expose to our view the fruits of religion. It is interesting to compare the restraint of this method with that of certain more recent theorists. Some anthropologists and psychologists developed the habit of saying that since religion begins with fear or repression or something of the sort, and since it can be shown to have bad effects upon "personality (or social) development" it must be false. This was not Hume's way. He gives us what he takes to be all the relevant facts, or at least a representative selection of all the facts. After all, this is what a natural history ought to do. There is no need to go on and pronounce upon the truth or falsity of that thing which the facts display. They tell their own story. They tell us no more and no less than what religion really is. It is of course possible to enquire into the rational foundation of any specific belief, but to do this is to do philosophy and not natural history.

Perhaps it was this detachment, this natural historian's attitude toward religion which most enraged Hume's orthodox contemporaries. It was one thing to argue philosophically about religion with an unbeliever. But to treat sacred matters with such a heavy hand, to presume to deal with religion as impersonally as one might deal with any sort of belief or practice seemed in itself sacrilegious. Most of us are not longer sensitive in quite this way or to quite this degree. We have grown used to the idea that it is legitimate to treat religion in an objective or scientific way. The comparative study of religions has now become a recognized part of the discipline of theology, and although its productions little resemble the work of Hume few would deny it the right to assume a detached attitude when it deals with the data of religion.

If we are dissatisfied with the plan or the theories or the conclusions of *The Natural History of Religion*, we shall probably be dissatisfied in another way. It is not that Hume chooses to bring out the character of religion by enumerating certain facts of religious practice and belief. To deny the propriety of this method would be to deny the relevance of facts to our estimate of the nature of value of religion. Rather it is his arrangement and selection of the facts which may seem inadequate. There is no question here of Hume's philosophical sincerity and honesty. There may well be a question about his objectivity and about the limitations of his insight. Clearly we can no longer take his authorities, classical authors, and the world-travellers of the eighteenth century quite so seriously as Hume took them. Their evidence, even under the most generous historical canons, can hardly be regarded as well sifted or thoroughly authenticated. (This is not to maintain that it would be impossible today to write an account of religion of the same tenor as Hume's, that is by making use of evidence more fully authenticated. But the facts would be different facts and they would be differently attested.) The flaws in Hume's factual material are not the most serious matter. A far more serious thing is the disquieting sameness of all the illustrations. Even though the stories are often extraordinary and sometimes amusing, they are always extraordinary in exactly the same way. The picture of religion which results is certainly not dull but it is depressingly uniform. It is not surprising to find that the chosen facts and illustrations neatly support the theories of *The Natural History of Religion*, but a consequence of this neatness is that religion as a whole is made to look monochrome and suspiciously homogeneous. It is one thing to construct a theory to account for such facts as *The Natural History of Religion* presents, but as in the case of many theories (especially philosophical and theological ones) we must beware lest the theory blind us to the actual multiplicity of facts which may be there and to the many-sided qualities of that thing which we are seeking to understand. It is not only conceivable but highly probable that some of the facts will never fit into those ready-made pigeon-holes where we would be so glad to put them. In other words a monochrome picture of religion, whether painted by the pious or the sceptical, is always likely to be a distorted picture. Or to put it in still another way, the loose ends, the facts which seem to fit nowhere as far as the theory is concerned, are as much a part of the whole story as the facts which slip easily into place. The extent of our insight is to some degree measured by whether we are or are not willing to block our vision in the interests of theoretical consistency.

This perhaps is a source of our dissatisfaction with Hume's account, for we look in vain for some features of religious belief and practice which he seems never to have noticed. It is perfectly true that unreasonable hopes and fears and extravagant superstition and credulity have played and continue to play a part in the religious behaviour of mankind. It is quite obvious that bigotry and fanaticism, allegedly inspired by religious belief, have often been behind deeds which many religious men would like to forget. All of these *The Natural History of Religion* explores at length. It does not tell us much about the trust, the kindness, the charity and indeed the reasonableness which are also to be seen as fruits of religion. It does not tell us, in fact, all sorts of things which we want to know before we can happily accept any theory of what religion really *is*. Hume rightly saw that a description of religion should include a report of both religious practices and beliefs and their consequences in ordinary life. It could never be easy to measure the full consequences of religious belief, but we may be misled because those consequences which offend conventional

morality are the ones we notice first. It is dangerous to argue
from obviousness to ubiquity or to suppose that what we notice first
is of the first importance. Nothing is easier than to see and condemn
heresy hunts, witch burnings, and wars of persecution. It is another
thing to appraise rightly those manifold fruits of the Spirit which
religious people not uncommonly but not so dramatically exhibit.
Hume saw religion as the sum total of its manifestations. One wonders
what he would have said to the claim that it can be better described as
a "way of life" or as a complex of attitudes not quite identical with those
individual beliefs and practices in which it variously finds expression.
He did find one basic attitude: fear. But this alone seems scarcely
adequate for making sense of some of those facts which Hume neglects
to lay before us. Compared with the sharpness and clarity of *The
Natural History of Religion* any account which made use of such a
phrase as "way of life" might seem hopelessly vague and fuzzy. But
if empirical accounts of religion cannot cope with inconvenient facts
and cannot admit that there are fuzzy edges here and there, then
empiricism itself is being sacrificed to some hidden principles which
have little to do with what we behold when our eyes are open.

This sort of question may lead us to wonder whether rather special
qualifications are needed by the natural historian of something so
complex as the phenomena of religion. It would not be fair to blame
Hume for lack of sympathy with religion as he understood it, and
certainly we find in him little of that "concern" which has characterized
much of the most perceptive writing, whether by believers or un-
believers, on the nature of religion. It may be that there are questions,
and questions in religion and in metaphysics might be examples, where
the most illuminating discussions come only from those who are not so
anxious to dispose of them as to understand them in all their complex-
ity, and to do this as enquirers who are personally moved and involved
in these perplexities and complications. In an unexpected but very
enlightening comparison between the work and influence of Hume and
Wesley, John Oman once wrote: ". . . the thing which perhaps not
merely Hume himself but his philosophy most needed was some kind
of conversion." This may be asking for too much or it may be asking
for the wrong thing. The unconverted and the not-quite-converted
can make valuable contributions to our understanding. But the
comment does put in religious words something of the nature of the

complaints which now, after two hundred years, some will still wish to make against *The Natural History of Religion*. The comment has an added importance in that it comes from perhaps the most distinguished "natural historian" of religion of recent times.

It cannot be denied that religion influences individuals and groups and that it changes lives, but there is no law of nature which proclaims that the change must always be one for the worse. Hume seems curiously insensitive to the fact that even "popular" religion produces saints. (The allusion to a Christian saint, in Sect. X, gives us no grounds for supposing that he believed religion could ever be ennobling.) This insensitivity, and some might prefer a less generous word, is extremely hard to explain. Even if we fully allow for the unhappy influence of the bleak Calvinism of eighteenth century Scotland upon Hume's ideas, he must have known some men whose religion was hardly covered by the account in *The Natural History of Religion*. The fact is that he did know such men and counted as friends a group of "Moderate" Presbyterian clergy. Perhaps the explanation is that for Hume their religion was not *real* religion but something else. And what then was the religion of a St. Francis of Assisi, *real* religion or some other thing?

All of this may point to limitations in Hume's work, but feelings of dissatisfaction in no way count against either the historical importance or the present usefulness of *The Natural History of Religion*. It is not a bad thing that people who are more sympathetic with the religious impulse should be shown some of the facts which they tend to ignore. Hume does this in good humour and, at least in some ways, with restraint. He explores almost to their limits certain provinces of religious life and belief which are very much a part of the whole story. With the singleness of mind appropriate, one might say, to the metaphysician or theologian he arranges the facts in that order which most perspicuously displays what he takes the nature of religion to be. If we find it defective, this is like the feeling we have when, as jurors, we know that counsel for the prosecution has presented his case brilliantly and counsel for the defence has been dull. It is not that we wish the prosecution had been duller but that we wish the defence had been less so. Whether our hope to see religion with greater insight can be fulfilled or not, *The Natural History of Religion*, as the best example of one possible approach, can sharpen those contours of our apprehension which, through prejudice or dullness, we might otherwise leave untended.

In his concluding pages and in perhaps the best-known passage in the work, Hume determines to abandon speculation about religion and theology, retiring to the cooler climate of philosophy. Philosophers who came after Hume tended to suppose that philosophy could provide a reasonable and satisfactory substitute for religion. But these days philosophers have given up all attempts to offer their wares as substitutes for theologies or moralisms. It is not without interest that this new attitude owes a great deal to Hume's influence. What then are we to make of Hume's last exit? Philosophy, however therapeutic, cannot and does not propose to create for us that pure and aseptic mental atmosphere where we can forget the human scene and tend our gardens or play chess without interruption. Whether to our salvation or damnation we will have to go on doing theology. And ironic as it may seem, Hume will help us to do it better than we should have done it without him.

H. E. Root.

AUTHOR'S INTRODUCTION

As every enquiry, which regards religion, is of the utmost importance, there are two questions in particular, which challenge our attention, to wit, that concerning its foundation in reason, and that concerning its origin in human nature. Happily, the first question, which is the most important, admits of the most obvious, at least, the clearest, solution. The whole frame of nature bespeaks an intelligent author; and no rational enquirer can, after serious reflection, suspend his belief a moment with regard to the primary principles of genuine Theism and Religion. But the other question, concerning the origin of religion in human nature, is exposed to some more difficulty. The belief of invisible, intelligent power has been very generally diffused over the human race, in all places and in all ages; but it has neither perhaps been so universal as to admit of no exception, nor has it been, in any degree, uniform in the ideas, which it has suggested. Some nations have been discovered, who entertained no sentiments of Religion, if travellers and historians may be credited; and no two nations, and scarce any two men, have ever agreed precisely in the same sentiments. It would appear, therefore, that this preconception springs not from an original instinct or primary impression of nature, such as gives rise to self-love, affection between the sexes, love of progeny, gratitude, resentment; since every instinct of this kind has been found absolutely universal in all nations and ages, and has always a precise determinate object, which it inflexibly pursues. The first religious principles must be secondary; such as may easily be perverted by various accidents and causes, and whose operation too, in some cases, may, by an extraordinary concurrence of circumstances, be altogether prevented. What those principles are, which give rise to the original belief, and what those accidents and causes are, which direct its operation, is the subject of our present enquiry.

I

THAT POLYTHEISM WAS THE PRIMARY
RELIGION OF MAN

It appears to me, that, if we consider the improvement of human society, from rude beginnings to a state of greater perfection, polytheism or idolatry was, and necessarily must have been, the first and most ancient religion of mankind. This opinion I shall endeavour to confirm by the following arguments.

It is a matter of fact incontestable, that about 1,700 years ago all mankind were polytheists. The doubtful and sceptical principles of a few philosophers, or the theism, and that too not entirely pure, of one or two nations, form no objection worth regarding. Behold then the clear testimony of history. The farther we mount up into antiquity, the more do we find mankind plunged into polytheism. No marks, no symptoms of any more perfect religion. The most ancient records of human race still present us with that system as the popular and established creed. The north, the south, the east, the west, give their unanimous testimony to the same fact. What can be opposed to so full an evidence?

As far as writing or history reaches, mankind, in ancient times, appear universally to have been polytheists. Shall we assert, that, in more ancient times, before the knowledge of letters, or the discovery of any art or science, men entertained the principles of pure theism? That is, while they were ignorant and barbarous, they discovered truth: But fell into error, as soon as they acquired learning and politeness.

But in this assertion you not only contradict all appearance of probability, but also our present experience concerning the principles and opinions of barbarous nations. The savage tribes of AMERICA, AFRICA, and ASIA are all idolaters. Not a single exception to this rule. Insomuch, that, were a traveller to transport himself into any unknown region; if he found inhabitants cultivated with arts and science, though even upon that supposition there are odds against their being theists, yet could he not safely, till farther inquiry, pronounce any thing on that head: But if he found them ignorant and barbarous, he might beforehand declare them idolaters; and there scarcely is a possibility of his being mistaken.

It seems certain, that, according to the natural progress of human thought, the ignorant multitude must first entertain some groveling and familiar notion of superior powers, before they stretch their conception to that perfect Being, who bestowed order on the whole frame of nature. We may as reasonably imagine, that men inhabited palaces before huts and cottages, or studied geometry before agriculture; as assert that the Deity appeared to them a pure spirit, omniscient, omnipotent, and omnipresent, before he was apprehended to be a powerful, though limited being, with human passions and appetites, limbs and organs. The mind rises gradually, from inferior to superior: By abstracting from what is imperfect, it forms an idea of perfection: And slowly distinguishing the nobler parts of its own frame from the grosser, it learns to transfer only the former, much elevated and refined, to its divinity. Nothing could disturb this natural progress of thought, but some obvious and invincible argument, which might immediately lead the mind into the pure principles of theism, and make it overleap, at one bound, the vast interval which is interposed between the human and the divine nature. But though I allow, that the order and frame of the universe, when accurately examined, affords such an argument; yet I can never think, that this consideration could have an influence on mankind, when they formed their first rude notions of religion.

The causes of such objects, as are quite familiar to us, never strike our attention or curiosity; and however extraordinary or surprising these objects in themselves, they are passed over, by the raw and ignorant multitude, without much examination or enquiry. ADAM, rising at once, in paradise, and in the full perfection of his faculties, would naturally, as represented by MILTON, be astonished at the glorious appearances of nature, the heavens, the air, the earth, his own organs and members; and would be led to ask, whence this wonderful scene arose. But a barbarous, necessitous animal (such as a man is on the first origin of society), pressed by such numerous wants and passions, has no leisure to admire the regular face of nature, or make enquiries concerning the cause of those objects, to which from his infancy he has been gradually accustomed. On the contrary, the more regular and uniform, that is, the more perfect nature appears, the more is he familiarized to it, and the less inclined to scrutinize and examine it. A monstrous birth excites his curiosity, and is deemed a prodigy. It alarms him from its novelty; and immediately sets him a trembling, and sacrificing, and praying. But an animal, compleat in all its limbs and organs, is to him an ordinary spectacle, and produces no religious opinion or affection. Ask him, whence that animal arose; he will tell you, from the copulation of its parents. And these, whence? From the copulation of theirs. A few removes satisfy his curiosity, and set the objects at such a distance, that he entirely loses sight of them. Imagine not, that he will so much as start the question, whence the first animal; much less, whence the whole system, or united fabric of the universe arose. Or, if you start such a question to him, expect not, that he will employ his mind with any anxiety about a subject, so remote, so uninteresting, and which so much exceeds the bounds of his capacity.

But farther, if men were at first led into the belief of one Supreme Being, by reasoning from the frame of nature, they could never possibly leave that belief, in order to embrace polytheism; but the same principles of reason, which at first produced and diffused over mankind, so magnificent an opinion, must be able, with greater facility, to preserve it. The first invention and proof of any doctrine is much more difficult than the supporting and retaining of it.

There is a great difference between historical facts and speculative opinions; nor is the knowledge of the one propagated in the same manner with that of the other. An historical fact, while it passes by oral tradition from eyewitnesses and contemporaries, is disguised in every successive narration, and may at last retain but very small, if any, resemblance of the original truth, on which it was founded. The frail memories of men, their love of exaggeration, their supine carelessness; these principles, if not corrected by books and writing, soon pervert the account of historical events; where argument or reasoning has little or no place, nor can ever recal the truth, which has once escaped those narrations. It is thus the fables of HERCULES, THESEUS, BACCHUS are supposed to have been originally founded in true history, corrupted by tradition. But with regard to speculative opinions, the case is far otherwise. If these opinions be founded on arguments so clear and obvious as to carry conviction with the generality of mankind, the same arguments, which at first diffused the opinions, will still preserve them in their original purity. If the arguments be more abstruse, and more remote from vulgar apprehension, the opinions will always be confined to a few persons; and as soon as men leave the contemplation of the arguments, the opinions will immediately be lost and be buried in oblivion. Whichever side of this dilemma we take, it must appear impossible, that theism could, from reasoning, have been the primary religion of human race, and have afterwards, by its corruption, given birth to polytheism and to all the various superstitions of the heathen world. Reason, when obvious, prevents these corruptions: When abstruse, it keeps the principles entirely from the knowledge of the vulgar, who are alone liable to corrupt any principle or opinion.

II

ORIGIN OF POLYTHEISM

If we would, therefore, indulge our curiosity, in enquiring concerning the origin of religion, we must turn our thoughts towards polytheism, the primitive religion of uninstructed mankind.

Were men led into the apprehension of invisible, intelligent power by a contemplation of the works of nature, they could never possibly entertain any conception but of one single being, who bestowed existence and order on this vast machine, and adjusted all its parts, according to one regular plan or connected system. For though, to persons of a certain turn of mind, it may not appear altogether absurd, that several independent beings, endowed with superior wisdom, might conspire in the contrivance and execution of one regular plan; yet is this a merely arbitrary supposition, which, even if allowed possible, must be confessed neither to be supported by probability nor necessity. All things in the universe are evidently of a piece. Every thing is adjusted to every thing. One design prevails throughout the whole. And this uniformity leads the mind to acknowledge one author; because the conception of different authors, without any distinction of attributes or operations, serves only to give perplexity to the imagination, without bestowing any satisfaction on the understanding. The statue of LAOCOON, as we learn from PLINY, was the work of three artists: But it is certain, that, were we not told so, we should never have imagined, that a groupe of figures, cut from one stone, and united in one plan, was not the work and contrivance of one statuary. To ascribe any single effect to the combination of several causes, is not surely a natural and obvious supposition.

On the other hand, if, leaving the works of nature, we trace the footsteps of invisible power in the various and contrary events of human life, we are necessarily led into polytheism and to the acknowledgment of several limited and imperfect deities. Storms and tempests ruin what is nourished by the sun. The sun destroys what is fostered by the moisture of dews and rains. War may be favourable to a nation, whom the inclemency of the seasons afflicts with famine, Sickness and pestilence may depopulate a kingdom, amidst the most profuse plenty. The same nation is not, at the same time, equally successful by sea and by land. And a nation, which now triumphs over its enemies, may anon submit to their more prosperous arms. In short, the conduct of events, or what we call the plan of a particular providence, is so full of variety and uncertainty, that, if we suppose it immediately ordered by any intelligent beings, we must acknowledge a contrariety in their designs and intentions, a constant combat of opposite powers, and a repentance or change of intention in the same power, from impotence or levity. Each nation has its tutelar deity. Each element is subjected to its invisible power or agent. The province of each god is separate from that of another. Nor are the operations of the same god always certain and invariable. To-day he protects: To-morrow he abandons us. Prayers and sacrifices, rites and ceremonies, well or ill performed, are the sources of his favour or enmity, and produce all the good or ill fortune, which are to be found amongst mankind.

We may conclude, therefore, that, in all nations, which have embraced polytheism, the first ideas of religion arose not from a contemplation of the works of nature, but from a concern with regard to the events of life, and from the incessant hopes and fears, which actuate the human mind. Accordingly, we find, that all idolaters, having separated the provinces of their deities, have recourse to that invisible agent, to whose authority they are immediately subjected, and whose province it is to superintend that course of actions, in which they are, at any time, engaged. JUNO is invoked at marriages; LUCINA at births. NEPTUNE receives the prayers of seamen; and MARS of warriors. The husbandman cultivates his field under the protection of

CERES; and the merchant acknowledges the authority of MERCURY. Each natural event is supposed to be governed by some intelligent agent; and nothing prosperous or adverse can happen in life, which may not be the subject of peculiar prayers or thanksgivings.[1]

It must necessarily, indeed, be allowed, that, in order to carry men's intention beyond the present course of things, or lead them into any inference concerning invisible intelligent power, they must be actuated by some passion, which prompts their thought and reflection; some motive, which urges their first enquiry. But what passion shall we here have recourse to, for explaining an effect of such mighty consequences? Not speculative curiosity, surely, or the pure love of truth. That motive is too refined for such gross apprehensions; and would lead men into enquiries concerning the frame of nature, a subject too large and comprehensive for their narrow capacities. No passions, therefore, can be supposed to work upon such barbarians, but the ordinary affections of human life; the anxious concern for happiness, the dread of future misery, the terror of death, the thirst of revenge, the appetite for food and other necessaries. Agitated by hopes and fears of this nature, especially the latter, men scrutinize, with a trembling curiosity, the course of future causes, and examine the various and contrary events of human life. And in this disordered scene, with eyes still more disordered and astonished, they see the first obscure traces of divinity.

III

THE SAME SUBJECT CONTINUED

We are placed in this world, as in a great theatre, where the true springs and causes of every event are entirely concealed from us; nor have we either sufficient wisdom to foresee, or power to prevent those ills, with which we are continually threatened. We hang in perpetual

---

[1] 'Fragilis & laboriosa mortalitas in partes ista digessit, infirmitatis suae memor, ut portionibus coleret quisque, quo maxime iudigeret.' PLIN. lib. ii. cap. 5. So early as Hesiod's time there were 30,000 deities. *Oper. & Dier.* lib. i. ver. 250. But the task to be performed by these seems still too great for their number. The provinces of the deities were so subdivided, that there was even a God of *Sneezing*. See ARIST. *Probl.* sect. 33. cap. 7. The province of copulation, suitably to the importance and dignity of it, was divided among several deities.

suspence between life and death, health and sickness, plenty and want; which are distributed amongst the human species by secret and unknown causes, whose operation is oft unexpected, and always unaccountable. These *unknown causes*, then, become the constant object of our hope and fear; and while the passions are kept in perpetual alarm by an anxious expectation of the events, the imagination is equally employed in forming ideas of those powers, on which we have so entire a dependance. Could men anatomize nature, according to the most probable, at least the most intelligible philosophy, they would find, that these causes are nothing but the particular fabric and structure of the minute parts of their own bodies and of external objects; and that, by a regular and constant machinery, all the events are produced, about which they are so much concerned. But this philosophy exceeds the comprehension of the ignorant multitude, who can only conceive the *unknown causes* in a general and confused manner; though their imagination, perpetually employed on the same subject, must labour to form some particular and distinct idea of them. The more they consider these causes themselves, and the uncertainty of their operation, the less satisfaction do they meet with in their researches; and, however unwilling, they must at last have abandoned so arduous an attempt, were it not for a propensity in human nature, which leads into a system, that gives them some satisfaction.

There is an universal tendency among mankind to conceive all beings like themselves, and to transfer to every object, those qualities, with which they are familiarly acquainted, and of which they are intimately conscious. We find human faces in the moon, armies in the clouds; and by a natural propensity, if not corrected by experience and reflection, ascribe malice or good-will to every thing, that hurts or pleases us. Hence the frequency and beauty of the *prosopopœia* in poetry; where trees, mountains and streams are personified, and the inanimate parts of nature acquire sentiment and passion. And though these poetical figures and expressions gain not on the belief, they may serve, at least, to prove a certain tendency in the imagination, without which they could neither be beautiful nor natural. Nor is a river-god or hamadryad always taken for a mere poetical or imaginary personage; but may sometimes enter into the real creed of the ignorant vulgar; while each grove or field is represented as possessed of a particular *genius* or invisible power, which inhabits and protects it. Nay, philosophers cannot entirely exempt themselves from this natural frailty; but have oft ascribed it to inanimate matter the horror of a *vacuum*, sympathies, antipathies, and other affections of human nature. The absurdity is not less, while we cast our eyes upwards; and transferring, as is too usual, human passions and infirmities to the deity, represent him as jealous and revengeful, capricious and partial, and, in short, a wicked and foolish man, in every respect but his superior power and authority. No wonder, then, that mankind, being placed in such an absolute ignorance of causes, and being at the same time so anxious concerning their future fortune, should immediately acknowledge a dependence on invisible powers, possessed of sentiment and intelligence. The *unknown causes* which continually employ their thought, appearing always in the same aspect, are all apprehended to be of the same kind or species. Nor is it long before we ascribe to them thought and reason and passion, and sometimes even the limbs and figures of men, in order to bring them nearer to a resemblance with ourselves.

In proportion as any man's course of life is governed by accident, we always find, that he encreases in superstition; as may particularly be observed of gamesters and sailors, who, though, of all mankind, the least capable of serious reflection, abound most in frivolous and superstitious apprehensions. The gods, says CORIOLANUS in DIONYSIUS[1], have an influence in every affair; but above all, in war; where the event is so uncertain. All human life, especially before the institution of order and good government, being subject to fortuitous accidents; it is natural, that superstition should prevail every where in barbarous ages, and put men on the most earnest enquiry concerning those invisible powers, who dispose of their happiness or misery. Ignorant of astronomy and the anatomy of plants and animals, and too little curious to observe the admirable adjustment of final causes; they remain still unacquainted with a first and supreme creator, and with that infinitely perfect spirit, who alone, by his almighty will, bestowed order on the whole frame of nature. Such a magnificent idea is too big for their narrow conceptions, which can neither observe the beauty of the work, nor comprehend the grandeur of its author. They suppose their deities, however potent and invisible, to be nothing but a species of human creatures, perhaps raised from among mankind, and retaining all human passions and appetites, together with corporeal limbs and

1 Lib. viii. 33

organs. Such limited beings, though masters of human fate, being, each of them, incapable of extending his influence every where, must be vastly multiplied, in order to answer that variety of events, which happen over the whole face of nature. Thus every place is stored with a crowd of local deities; and thus polytheism has prevailed, and still prevails, among the greatest part of uninstructed mankind.[1]

Any of the human affections may lead us into the notion of invisible, intelligent power; hope as well as fear, gratitude as well as affliction: But if we examine our own hearts, or observe what passes around us, we shall find, that men are much oftener thrown on their knees by the melancholy than by the agreeable passions. Prosperity is easily received as our due, and few questions are asked concerning its cause or author. It begets cheerfulness and activity and alacrity and a lively enjoyment of every social and sensual pleasure: And during this state of mind, men have little leisure or inclination to think of the unknown invisible regions. On the other hand, every disastrous accident alarms us, and sets us on enquiries concerning the principles whence it arose: Apprehensions spring up with regard to futurity: And the mind, sunk into diffidence, terror, and melancholy, has recourse to every method of appeasing those secret intelligent powers, on whom our fortune is supposed entirely to depend.

No topic is more usual with all popular divines than to display the advantages of affliction, in bringing men to a due sense of religion; by subduing their confidence and sensuality, which, in times of prosperity, make them forgetful of a divine providence. Nor is this topic confined merely to modern religions. The ancients have also employed it. *Fortune has never liberally, without envy,* says a GREEK historian,[2] *bestowed an unmixed happiness on mankind; but with all her*

---

[1] The following lines of EURIPIDES are so much to the present purpose, that I cannot forbear quoting them:

Οὐκ ἔστιν οὐδὲν πιστὸν, οὔτ' εὐδοξία,
Οὔτ' αὖ καλῶς πράσσοντα μὴ πράξειν κακῶς.
Φύρουσι δ' αὖθ' οἱ θεοὶ πάλιν τε καὶ πρόσω,
Ταραγμὸν ἐντιθέντες, ὡς ἀγνωσίᾳ
Σέβωμεν αὐτούς.   HECUBA, 956.

'There is nothing secure in the world; no glory, no prosperity. The gods toss all life into confusion; mix every thing with its reverse; that all of us, from our ignorance and uncertainty, may pay them the more worship and reverence.'

[2] DIOD. SIC. lib. iii. 47.

gifts has ever conjoined some disastrous circumstance, in order to chastize men into a reverence for the gods, whom, in a continued course of prosperity, they are apt to neglect and forget.

What age or period of life is the most addicted to superstition? The weakest and most timid. What sex? The same answer must be given. *The leaders and examples of every kind of superstition,* says STRABO,[1] *are the women. These excite the men to devotion and supplications, and the observance of religious days. It is rare to meet with one that lives apart from the females, and yet is addicted to such practices.* And nothing can, for this reason, be more improbable, than the account given of an order of men among the GETES, who practised celibacy, and were notwithstanding the most religious fanatics. A method of reasoning, which would lead us to entertain a bad idea of the devotion of monks; did we not know by an experience, not so common, perhaps, in STRABO's days, that one may practise celibacy, and profess chastity; and yet maintain the closest connexions and most entire sympathy with that timorous and pious sex.

IV

DEITIES NOT CONSIDERED AS CREATORS OR FORMERS OF THE WORLD

The only point of theology, in which we shall find a consent of mankind almost universal, is, that there is invisible, intelligent power in the world: But whether this power be supreme or subordinate, whether confined to one being, or distributed among several, what attributes, qualities, connexions, or principles of action ought to be ascribed to those beings; concerning all these points, there is the widest difference in the popular systems of theology. Our ancestors in EUROPE, before the revival of letters, believed, as we do at present, that there was one supreme God, the author of nature, whose power, though in itself uncontroulable, was yet often exerted by the inter-position of his angels and subordinate ministers, who executed his sacred purposes. But they also believed, that all nature was full of other invisible powers; fairies, goblins, elves, sprights; beings, stronger and mightier than men, but much inferior to the celestial natures, who

[1] Lib. vi. 297.

surround the throne of God. Now, suppose, that any one, in those ages, had denied the existence of God and of his angels; would not his impiety justly have deserved the appellation of atheism, even though he had still allowed, by some odd capricious reasoning, that the popular stories of elves and fairies were just and well-grounded? The difference, on the one hand, between such a person and a genuine theist is infinitely greater than that, on the other, between him and one that absolutely excludes all invisible intelligent power. And it is a fallacy, merely from the casual resemblance of names, without any conformity of meaning, to rank such opposite opinions under the same denomination.

To any one, who considers justly of the matter, it will appear, that the gods of all polytheists are not better than the elves or fairies of our ancestors, and merit as little any pious worship or veneration. These pretended religionists are really a kind of superstitious atheists, and acknowledge no being, that corresponds to our idea of a deity. No first principle of mind or thought: No supreme government and administration: No divine contrivance or intention in the fabric of the world.

The CHINESE, when[1] their prayers are not answered, beat their idols. The deities of the LAPLANDERS are any large stone which they meet with of an extraordinary shape.[2] The EGYPTIAN mythologists, in order to account for animal worship, said, that the gods, pursued by the violence of earthborn men, who were their enemies, had formerly been obliged to disguise themselves under the semblance of beasts.[3] The CAUNII, a nation in the Lesser ASIA, resolving to admit no strange gods among them, regularly, at certain seasons, assembled themselves compleatly armed, beat the air with their lances, and proceeded in that manner to their frontiers; in order, as they said, to expel the foreign deities.[4] *Not even the immortal gods*, said some GERMAN nations to CÆSAR, *are a match for the* SUEVI.[5]

Many ills, says DIONE in HOMER to VENUS wounded by DIO-MEDE, many ills, my daughter, have the gods inflicted on men: And

[1] Pere le Compte.
[2] Regnard, Voïage de Laponie.
[3] Diod. Sic. lib. i. 86. Lucian. de Sacrificiis. 14. OVID alludes to the same tradition, Metam. lib. v. l. 321. So also MANILIUS, lib. iv. 800.
[4] Herodot. lib. i. 172.
[5] Caes. Comment. de bello Gallico, lib. iv. 7.

many ills, in return, have men inflicted on the gods.[1] We need but open any classic author to meet with these gross representations of the deities; and LONGINUS[2] with reason observes, that such ideas of the divine nature, if literally taken, contain a true atheism.

Some writers[3] have been surprized, that the impieties of ARISTO-PHANES should have been tolerated, nay publicly acted and applauded by the ATHENIANS; a people so superstitious and so jealous of the public religion, that, at that very time, they put SOCRATES to death for his imagined incredulity. But these writers do not consider, that the ludicrous, familiar images, under which the gods are represented by that comic poet, instead of appearing impious, were the genuine lights in which the ancients conceived their divinities. What conduct can be more criminal or mean, than that of JUPITER in the AMPHIT-RION? Yet that play, which represented his gallante exploits, was supposed so agreeable to him, that it was always acted in ROME by public authority, when the state was threatened with pestilence, famine, or any general calamity.[4] The ROMANS supposed, that, like all old letchers, he would be highly pleased with the recital of his former feats of prowess and vigour, and that no topic was so proper, upon which to flatter his vanity.

The LACEDEMONIANS, says XENOPHON,[5] always, during war, put up their petitions very early in the morning, in order to be before-hand with their enemies, and, by being the first solicitors, pre-engage the gods in their favour. We may gather from SENECA,[6] that it was usual, for the votaries in the temples, to make interest with the beadle or sexton, that they might have a seat near the image of the deity, in order to be the best heard in their prayers and applications to him. The TYRIANS, when beseiged by ALEXANDER, threw chains on the statue of HERCULES, to prevent that deity from deserting to the enemy.[7] AUGUSTUS, having twice lost his fleet by storms, forbad NEPTUNE to be carried in procession along with the other gods; and fancied, that he had sufficiently revenged himself by that expedient.[8] After GERMANICUS's death, the people were so enraged at their

[1] Lib. v. 382. [2] Cap. ix.
[3] Pere Brumoy, Theatre des Grecs; & Fontenelle, Histoire des Oracles.
[4] Arnob. lib. vii. 507 H. [5] De Laced. Rep. 13.
[6] Epist. xli.
[7] Quint. Curtius, lib. iv. cap. 3. Diod. Sic. lib. xvii. 41.
[8] Suet. in vita Aug. cap. 16.

gods, that they stoned them in their temples; and openly renounced all allegiance to them.[1]

To ascribe the origin and fabric of the universe to these imperfect beings never enters into the imagination of any polytheist or idolater. HESIOD, whose writings, with those of HOMER, contained the canonical system of the heavens;[2] HESIOD, I say, supposes gods and men to have sprung equally from the unknown powers of nature.[3] And throughout the whole theogony of that author, PANDORA is the only instance of creation or a voluntary production; and she too was formed by the gods merely from despight to PROMETHEUS, who had furnished men with stolen fire from the celestial regions.[4] The ancient mythologists, indeed, seem throughout to have rather embraced the idea of generation than that of creation or formation; and to have thence accounted for the origin of this universe.

OVID, who lived in a learned age, and had been instructed by philosophers in the principles of a divine creation or formation of the world; finding, that such an idea would not agree with the popular mythology, which he delivers, leaves it, in a manner, loose and detached from his system. *Quisquis fuit ille Deorum?*[5] Whichever of the gods it was, says he, that dissipated the chaos, and introduced order into the universe. It could neither be SATURN, he knew, nor JUPITER, nor NEPTUNE, nor any of the received deities of paganism. His theological system had taught him nothing upon that head; and he leaves the matter equally undetermined.

DIODORUS SICULUS,[6] beginning his work with an enumeration of the most reasonable opinions concerning the origin of the world, makes no mention of a deity or intelligent mind; though it is evident from his history, that he was much more prone to superstition than to irreligion. And in another passage,[7] talking of the ICHTHYOPHAGI, a nation in INDIA, he says, that, there being so great difficulty in accounting for their descent, we must conclude them to be *aborigines,* without any beginning of their generation, propagating their race from all eternity; as some of the physiologers, in treating of the origin of

[1] Id. in vita Cal. cap. 5.
[2] Herodot. lib. ii. 53. Lucian, *Jupiter confutatus, de luctu, Saturn, &c.*
[3] ' Ὡς ὁμόθεν γεγάασι θεοὶ θνητοί τ' ἄνθρωποι. Hes. Opera & Dies. l. 108.
[4] Theog. 1. 570.   [5] Metamorph. lib. i. l. 32.
[6] Lib. i. 6 *et seq.*   [7] Lib. iii. 20.

nature, have justly observed. 'But in such subjects as these,' adds the historian, 'which exceed all human capacity, it may well happen, that those, who discourse the most, know the least; reaching a specious appearance of truth in their reasonings, while extremely wide of the real truth and matter of fact.'

A strange sentiment in our eyes, to be embraced by a professed and zealous religionist![1] But it was merely by accident, that the question concerning the origin of the world did ever in ancient times enter into religious systems, or was treated of by theologers. The philosophers alone made profession of delivering systems of this kind; and it was pretty late too before these bethought themselves of having recourse to a mind of supreme intelligence, as the first cause of all. So far was it from being esteemed profane in those days to account for the origin of things without a deity, that THALES, ANAXIMENES, HERACLITUS, and others, who embraced that system of cosmogony, past unquestioned; while ANAXAGORAS, the first undoubted theist, among the philosophers, was perhaps the first that ever was accused of atheism.[2]

We are told by SEXTUS EMPIRICUS,[3] that EPICURUS, when a boy, reading with his preceptor these verses of HESIOD,

> Eldest of beings, *chaos* first arose ;
> Next *earth*, wide-stretch'd, the *seat* of all :

the young scholar first betrayed his inquisitive genius, by asking, *And chaos whence?* But was told by his preceptor, that he must have recourse

[1] The same author, who can thus account for the origin of the world without a Deity, esteems it impious to explain from physical causes, the common accidents of life, earthquakes, inundations, and tempests; and devoutly ascribes these to the anger of JUPITER or NEPTUNE. A plain proof, whence he derived his ideas of religion. See lib. xv. c. 48. p. 364. Ex edit. RHODOMANNI.

[2] It will be easy to give a reason, why THALES, ANAXIMANDER, and those early philosophers, who really were atheists, might be very orthodox in the pagan creed; and why ANAXAGORAS and SOCRATES, though real theists, must naturally, in ancient times, be esteemed impious. The blind, unguided powers of nature, if they could produce men, might also produce such beings as JUPITER and NEPTUNE, who being the most powerful, intelligent existences in the world, would be proper objects of worship. But where a supreme intelligence, the first cause of all, is admitted, these capricious beings, if they exist at all, must appear very subordinate and dependent, and consequently be excluded from the rank of deities. PLATO (de leg. lib. x. 886 D.) assigns this reason for the imputation thrown on ANAXAGORAS, namely, his denying the divinity of the stars, planets, and other created objects.

[3] Adversus MATHEM, lib. ix. 480.

to the philosophers for a solution of such questions. And from this hint EPICURUS left philology and all other studies, in order to betake himself to that science, whence alone he expected satisfaction with regard to these sublime subjects.

The common people were never likely to push their researches so far, or derive from reasoning their systems of religion; when philologers and mythologists, we see, scarcely ever discovered so much penetration. And even the philosophers, who discourse of such topics, readily assented to the grossest theory, and admitted the joint origin of gods and men from night and chaos: from fire, water, air, or whatever they established to be the ruling element.

Nor was it only on their first origin, that the gods were supposed dependent on the powers of nature. Throughout the whole period of their existence they were subjected to the dominion of fate or destiny. *Think of the force of necessity,* says AGRIPPA to the ROMAN people, *that force, to which even the gods must submit.*[1] And the Younger PLINY,[2] agreeably to this way of thinking, tells us, that amidst the darkness, horror, and confusion, which ensued upon the first eruption of VESUVIUS, several concluded, that all nature was going to wrack, and that gods and men were perishing in one common ruin.

It is great complaisance, indeed, if we dignify with the name of religion such an imperfect system of theology, and put it on a level with later systems, which are founded on principles more just and more sublime. For my part, I can scarcely allow the principles even of MARCUS AURELIUS, PLUTARCH, and some other *Stoics* and *Academics,* though much more refined than the pagan superstition, to be worthy of the honourable appellation of theism. For if the mythology of the heathens resemble the ancient EUROPEAN system of spiritual beings, excluding God and angels, and leaving only fairies and sprights; the creed of these philosophers may justly be said to exclude a deity, and to leave only angels and fairies.

[1] DIONYS. HALIC. lib. vi. 54
[2] Epist. lib. vi.

V

VARIOUS FORMS OF POLYTHEISM: ALLEGORY, HERO-WORSHIP

But it is chiefly our present business to consider the gross polytheism of the vulgar, and to trace all its various appearances, in the principles of human nature, whence they are derived.

Whoever learns by argument, the existence of invisible intelligent power, must reason from the admirable contrivance of natural objects, and must suppose the world to be the workmanship of that divine being, the original cause of all things. But the vulgar polytheist, so far from admitting that idea, deifies every part of the universe, and conceives all the conspicuous productions of nature, to be themselves so many real divinities. The sun, moon, and stars, are all gods according to his system: Fountains are inhabited by nymphs, and trees by hamadryads: Even monkeys, dogs, cats, and other animals often become sacred in his eyes, and strike him with a religious veneration. And thus, however strong men's propensity to believe invisible, intelligent power in nature, their propensity is equally strong to rest their attention on sensible, visible objects; and in order to reconcile these opposite inclinations, they are led to unite the invisible power with some visible object.

The distribution also of distinct provinces to the several deities is apt to cause some allegory, both physical and moral, to enter into the vulgar systems of polytheism. The god of war will naturally be represented as furious, cruel, and impetuous: The god of poetry as elegant, polite, and amiable: The god of merchandise, especially in early times, as thievish and deceitful. The allegories, supposed in HOMER and other mythologists, I allow, have often been so strained, that men of sense are apt entirely to reject them, and to consider them as the production merely of the fancy and conceit of critics and commentators. But that allegory really has place in the heathen mythology is undeniable even on the least reflection. CUPID the son of VENUS; the Muses the daughters of Memory; PROMETHEUS, the wise brother, and EPIMETHEUS the foolish; HYGIEIA or the goddess of health descended from ÆSCULAPIUS or the god of Physic: Who sees not, in these, and in many other instances, the plain traces of allegory? When a god is supposed to preside over any passion, event, or system of actions, it is almost unavoidable to give him a genealogy, attributes, and adventures, suitable to his supposed powers and influence; and to carry on that similitude and comparison, which is naturally so agreeable to the mind of man.

Allegories, indeed, entirely perfect, we ought not to expect as the productions of ignorance and superstition; there being no work of genius that requires a nicer hand, or has been more rarely executed with success. That *Fear* and *Terror* are the sons of MARS is just; but why by VENUS?[1] That *Harmony* is the daughter of VENUS is regular; but why by MARS?[2] That *Sleep* is the brother of *Death* is suitable; but why describe him as enamoured of one of the Graces?[3] And since the ancient mythologists fall into mistakes so gross and palpable, we have no reason surely to expect such refined and long-spun allegories, as some have endeavoured to deduce from their fictions.

LUCRETIUS was plainly seduced by the strong appearance of allegory, which is observable in the pagan fictions. He first addresses himself to VENUS as to that generating power, which animates, renews, and beautifies the universe: But is soon betrayed by the mythology into incoherencies, while he prays to that allegorical personage to appease the furies of her lover MARS: An idea not drawn from allegory, but from the popular religion, and which LUCRETIUS, as an EPICUREAN, could not consistently admit of.

The deities of the vulgar are so little superior to human creatures, that, where men are affected with strong sentiments of veneration or gratitude for any hero or public benefactor, nothing can be more natural than to convert him into a god, and fill the heavens, after this manner, with continual recruits from among mankind. Most of the divinities of the ancient world are supposed to have once been men, and to have been beholden for their *apotheosis* to the admiration and affection of the people. The real history of their adventures, corrupted by tradition, and elevated by the marvellous, became a plentiful source of fable; especially in passing through the hands of poets, allegorists, and priests, who successively improved upon the wonder and astonishment of the ignorant multitude.

1 HESIOD. Theog. l. 935.
2 Id. ibid. & PLUT. in vita PELOP. 19.
3 ILIAD. xiv. 267.

Painters too and sculptors came in for their share of profit in the sacred mysteries; and furnishing men with sensible representations of their divinities, whom they cloathed in human figures, gave great encrease to the public devotion, and determined its object. It was probably for want of these arts in rude and barbarous ages, that men deified plants, animals, and even brute, unorganized matter; and rather than be without a sensible object of worship, affixed divinity to such ungainly forms. Could any statuary of SYRIA, in early times, have formed a just figure of APOLLO, the conic stone, HELIOGABALUS, had never become the object of such profound adoration, and been received as a representation of the solar deity.[1]

STILPO was banished by the council of AREOPAGUS, for affirming that the MINERVA in the citadel was no divinity; but the workmanship of PHIDIAS, the sculptor.[2] What degree of reason must we expect in the religious belief of the vulgar in other nations; when ATHENIANS and AREOPAGITES could entertain such gross misconceptions?

These then are the general principles of polytheism, founded in human nature, and little or nothing dependent on caprice and accident. As the causes, which bestow happiness or misery, are, in general, very little known and very uncertain, our anxious concern endeavours to attain a determinate idea of them; and finds no better expedient than to represent them as intelligent voluntary agents, like ourselves; only somewhat superior in power and wisdom. The limited influence of these agents, and their great proximity to human weakness, introduce the various distribution and division of their authority; and thereby give rise to allegory. The same principles naturally deify mortals, superior in power, courage, or understanding, and produce hero-worship; together with fabulous history and mythological tradition, in all its wild and unaccountable forms. And as an invisible spiritual intelligence is an object too refined for vulgar apprehension, men naturally affix it to some sensible representation; such as either the more conspicuous parts of nature, or the statues, images, and pictures, which a more refined age forms of its divinities.

---

[1] HERODIAN. lib. v. 3, 10. JUPITER AMMON is represented by CURTIUS as a deity of the same kind, lib. iv. cap. 7. The ARABIANS and PESSINUNTIANS adored also shapeless unformed stones as their deity. ARNOB. lib. vi. 496 A. So much did their folly exceed that of the EGYPTIANS.
[2] DIOD. LAERT. lib. ii. 16.

Almost all idolaters, of whatever age or country, concur in these general principles and conceptions; and even the particular characters and provinces, which they assign to their deities, are not extremely different.[1] The GREEK and ROMAN travellers and conquerors, without much difficulty, found their own deities every where; and said, This is MERCURY, that VENUS; this MARS, that NEPTUNE; by whatever title the strange gods might be denominated. The goddess HERTHA of our SAXON ancestors seems to be no other, according to TACITUS,[2] than the *Mater Tellus*, of the ROMANS; and his conjecture was evidently just.

VI

ORIGIN OF THEISM FROM POLYTHEISM

The doctrine of one supreme deity, the author of nature, is very ancient, has spread itself over great and populous nations, and among them has been embraced by all ranks and conditions of men: But whoever thinks that it has owed its success to the prevalent force of those invincible reasons, on which it is undoubtedly founded, would show himself little acquainted with the ignorance and stupidity of the people, and their incurable prejudices in favour of their particular superstitions. Even at this day, and in EUROPE, ask any of the vulgar, why he believes in an omnipotent creator of the world; he will never mention the beauty of final causes, of which he is wholly ignorant: He will not hold out his hand, and bid you contemplate the suppleness and variety of joints in his fingers, their bending all one way, the counterpoise which they receive from the thumb, the softness and fleshy parts of the inside of his hand, with all the other circumstances, which render that member fit for the use, to which it was destined. To these he has been long accustomed; and he beholds them with listlessness and unconcern. He will tell you of the sudden and unexpected death of such a one: The fall and bruise of such another: The excessive drought of this season: The cold and rains of another. These he ascribes to the immediate operation of providence: And such events, as, with good reasoners, are the chief difficulties in admitting a supreme intelligence, are with him the sole arguments for it.

[1] See CÆSAR of the religion of the GAULS, De bello Gallico, lib. vi. 17.
[2] De moribus GERM. 40.

Many theists, even the most zealous and refined, have denied a *particular* providence, and have asserted, that the Sovereign mind or first principle of all things, having fixed general laws, by which nature is governed, gives free and uninterrupted course to these laws, and disturbs not, at every turn, the settled order of events by particular volitions. From the beautiful connexion, say they, and rigid observance of established rules, we draw the chief argument for theism; and from the same principles are enabled to answer the principal objections against it. But so little is this understood by the generality of mankind, that, wherever they observe any one to ascribe all events to natural causes, and to remove the particular interposition of a deity, they are apt to suspect him of the grossest infidelity. *A little philosophy*, says lord BACON, *makes men atheists: A great deal reconciles them to religion.* For men, being taught, by superstitious prejudices, to lay the stress on a wrong place; when that fails them, and they discover, by a little reflection, that the course of nature is regular and uniform, their whole faith totters, and falls to ruin. But being taught, by more reflection, that this very regularity and uniformity is the strongest proof of design and of a supreme intelligence, they return to that belief, which they had deserted; and they are now able to establish it on a firmer and more durable foundation.

Convulsions in nature, disorders, prodigies, miracles, though the most opposite to the plan of a wise superintendent, impress mankind with the strongest sentiments of religion; the causes of events seeming then the most unknown and unaccountable. Madness, fury, rage, and an inflamed imagination, though they sink men nearest to the level of beasts, are, for a like reason, often supposed to be the only dispositions, in which we can have any immediate communication with the Deity.

We may conclude, therefore, upon the whole, that, since the vulgar, in nations, which have embraced the doctrine of theism, still build it upon irrational and superstitious principles, they are never led into that opinion by any process of argument, but by a certain train of thinking, more suitable to their genius and capacity.

It may readily happen, in an idolatrous nation, that though men admit the existence of several limited deities, yet is there some one God, whom, in a particular manner, they make the object of their worship and adoration. They may either suppose, that, in the distribution of power and territory among the gods, their nation was subjected to the jurisdiction of that particular deity; or reducing heavenly objects to the model of things below, they may represent one god as the prince or supreme magistrate of the rest, who, though of the same nature, rules them with an authority, like that which an earthly sovereign exercises over his subjects and vassals. Whether this god, therefore, be considered as their peculiar patron, or as the general sovereign of heaven, his votaries will endeavour, by every art, to insinuate themselves into his favour; and supposing him to be pleased, like themselves, with praise and flattery, there is no eulogy or exaggeration, which will be spared in their addresses to him. In proportion as men's fears or distresses become more urgent, they still invent new strains of adulation; and even he who outdoes his predecessor in swelling up the titles of his divinity, is sure to be outdone by his successor in newer and more pompous epithets of praise. Thus they proceed; till at last they arrive at infinity itself, beyond which there is no farther progress: And it is well, if, in striving to get farther, and to represent a magnificent simplicity, they run not into inexplicable mystery, and destroy the intelligent nature of their deity, on which alone any rational worship or adoration can be founded. While they confine themselves to the notion of a perfect being, the creator of the world, they coincide, by chance, with the principles of reason and true philosophy; though they are guided to that notion, not by reason, of which they are in a great measure incapable, but by the adulation and fears of the most vulgar superstition.

We often find, amongst barbarous nations, and even sometimes amongst civilized, that, when every strain of flattery has been exhausted towards arbitrary princes, when every human quality has been applauded to the utmost; their servile courtiers represent them, at last, as real divinities, and point them out to the people as objects of adoration. How much more natural, therefore, is it, that a limited deity, who at first supposed only the immediate author of the particular goods and ills in life, should in the end be represented as sovereign maker and modifier of the universe?

Even where this notion of a supreme deity is already established; though it ought naturally to lessen every other worship, and abase every object of reverence, yet if a nation has entertained the opinion of a subordinate tutelar divinity, saint, or angel; their addresses to that being gradually rise upon them, and encroach on the adoration due to their supreme deity. The Virgin Mary, ere checked by the reformation, had proceeded, from being merely a good woman, to usurp many attributes of the Almighty: God and St NICHOLAS go hand in hand, in all the prayers and petitions of the MUSCOVITES.

Thus the deity, who, from love, converted himself into a bull, in order to carry off EUROPA; and who, from ambition, dethroned his father, SATURN, became the OPTIMUS MAXIMUS of the heathens. Thus, the God of ABRAHAM, ISAAC, and JACOB, became the supreme deity or JEHOVAH of the JEWS.

The JACOBINS, who denied the immaculate conception, have ever been very unhappy in their doctrine, even though political reasons have kept the ROMISH church from condemning it. The CORDEL-IERS have run away with all the popularity. But in the fifteenth century, as we learn from BOULAINVILLIERS,[1] an ITALIAN Cordelier maintained, that, during the three days, when CHRIST was interred, the hypostatic union was dissolved, and that his human nature was not a proper object of adoration, during that period. Without the art of divination, one might fortel, that so gross and impious a blasphemy would not fail to be anathematized by the people. It was the occasion of great insults on the part of the JACOBINS; who now got some recompense for their misfortunes in the war about the immaculate conception.

Rather than relinquish this propensity to adulation, religionists, in all ages, have involved themselves in the greatest absurdities and contradictions.

HOMER, in one passage, calls OCEANUS and TETHYS the original parents of all things, conformably to the established mythology and tradition of the GREEKS: Yet, in other passages, he could not forbear complimenting JUPITER, the reigning deity, with that magnificent appellation; and accordingly denominates him the father of gods and men. He forgets, that every temple, every street was full of the ancestors, uncles, brothers, and sisters of this JUPITER; who was in reality nothing but an upstart parricide and usurper. A like contradiction is observable in HESIOD; and is so much the less excusable, as his professed intention was to deliver a true genealogy of the gods.

Were there a religion (and we may suspect Mahometanism of this

1 Histoire abrégée, p. 499.

inconsistence) which sometimes painted the Deity in the most sublime colours, as the creator of heaven and earth; sometimes degraded him nearly to the level with human creatures in his powers and faculties; while at the same time it ascribed to him suitable infirmities, passions, and partialities, of the moral kind: That religion, after it was extinct, would also be cited as an instance of those contradictions, which arise from the gross, vulgar, natural conceptions of mankind, opposed to their continual propensity towards flattery and exaggeration. Nothing indeed would prove more strongly the divine origin of any religion, than to find (and happily this is the case with Christianity) that it is free from a contradiction, so incident to human nature.

VII

CONFIRMATION OF THIS DOCTRINE

It appears certain, that, though the original notions of the vulgar represent the Divinity as a limited being, and consider him only as the particular cause of health or sickness; plenty or want; prosperity or adversity; yet when more magnificent ideas are urged upon them, they esteem it dangerous to refuse their assent. Will you say, that your deity is finite and bounded in his perfections; may be overcome by a greater force; is subject to human passions, pains, and infirmities; has a beginning, and may have an end? This they dare not affirm; but thinking it safest to comply with the higher encomiums, they endeavour, by an affected ravishment and devotion, to ingratiate themselves with him. As a confirmation of this, we may observe, that the assent of the vulgar is, in this case, merely verbal, and that they are incapable of conceiving those sublime qualities, which they seemingly attribute to the Deity. Their real idea of him, notwithstanding their pompous language, is still as poor and frivolous as ever.

That original intelligence, say the MAGIANS, who is the first principle of all things, discovers himself *immediately* to the mind and understanding alone; but has placed the sun as his image in the visible universe; and when that bright luminary diffuses its beams over the earth and the firmament, it is a faint copy of the glory, which resides in the higher heavens. If you would escape the displeasure of this divine being, you must be careful never to set your bare foot upon the ground, nor spit into a fire, nor throw any water upon it, even though it were consuming a whole city.[1] Who can express the perfections of the Almighty? say the Mahometans. Even the noblest of his works, if compared to him, are but dust and rubbish. How much more must human conception fall short of his infinite perfections? His smile and favour renders men for ever happy; and to obtain it for your children, the best method is to cut off from them, while infants, a little bit of skin, about half the breadth of a farthing. Take two bits of cloth,[2] say the *Roman catholics*, about an inch or an inch and a half square, join them by the corners with two strings or pieces of tape about sixteen inches long, throw this over your head, and make one of the bits of cloth lie upon your breast, and the other upon your back, keeping them next your skin: There is not a better secret for recommending yourself to that infinite Being, who exists from eternity to eternity.

The GETES, commonly called immortal, from their steady belief of the soul's immortality, were genuine theists and unitarians. They affirmed ZAMOLXIS, their deity, to be the only true god; and asserted the worship of all other nations to be addressed to mere fictions and chimeras. But were their religious principles any more refined, on account of these magnificent pretensions? Every fifth year they sacrificed a human victim, whom they sent as a messenger to their deity, in order to inform him of their wants and necessities. And when it thundered, they were so provoked, that, in order to return the defiance, they let fly arrows at him, and declined not the combat as unequal. Such at least is the account, which HERODOTUS gives of the theism of the immortal GETES.[3]

VIII

FLUX AND REFLUX OF POLYTHEISM AND THEISM

It is remarkable, that the principles of religion have a kind of flux and reflux in the human mind, and that men have a natural tendency

---

[1] HYDE de Relig. veterum PERSARUM.
[2] Called the Scapulaire.   [3] Lib. iv. 94.

to rise from idolatry to theism, and to sink again from theism into idolatry. The vulgar, that is, indeed, all mankind, a few excepted, being ignorant and uninstructed, never elevate their contemplation to the heavens, or penetrate by their disquisitions into the secret structure of vegetable or animal bodies; so far as to discover a supreme mind or original providence, which bestowed order on every part of nature. They consider these admirable works in a more confined and selfish view; and finding their own happiness and misery to depend on the secret influence and unforeseen concurrence of external objects, they regard, with perpetual attention, the *unknown causes*, which govern all these natural events, and distribute pleasure and pain, good and ill, by their powerful, but silent, operation. The unknown causes are still appealed to on every emergence; and in this general appearance or confused image, are the perpetual objects of human hopes and fears, wishes and apprehensions. By degrees, the active imagination of men, uneasy in this abstract conception of objects, about which it is incessantly employed, begins to render them more particular, and to clothe them in shapes more suitable to its natural comprehension. It represents them to be sensible, intelligent beings, like mankind; actuated by love and hatred, and flexible by gifts and entreaties, by prayers and sacrifices. Hence the origin of religion: And hence the origin of idolatry or polytheism.

But the same anxious concern for happiness, which begets the idea of these invisible, intelligent powers, allows not mankind to remain long in the first simple conception of them; as powerful, but limited beings; masters of human fate, but slaves to destiny and the course of nature. Men's exaggerated praises and compliments still swell their idea upon them; and elevating their deities to the utmost bounds of perfection, at last beget the attributes of unity and infinity, simplicity and spirituality. Such refined ideas, being somewhat disproportioned to vulgar comprehension, remain not long in their original purity; but require to be supported by the notion of inferior mediators or subordinate agents, which interpose between mankind and their supreme deity. These demi-gods or middle beings, partaking more of human nature, and being more familiar to us, become the chief objects of devotion, and gradually recal that idolatry, which had been formerly banished by the ardent prayers and panegyrics of timorous and indigent mortals. But as these idolatrous religions fall every day into grosser and more vulgar conceptions, they at last destroy themselves, and by the vile representations, which they form of their deities, make the tide turn again towards theism. But so great is the propensity, in this alternate revolution of human sentiments, to return back to idolatry, that the utmost precaution is not able effectually to prevent it. And of this, some theists, particularly the JEWS and MAHOMETANS, have been sensible; as appears by their banishing all the arts of statuary and painting, and not allowing the representations, even of human figures, to be taken by marble or colours; lest the common informity of mankind should thence produce idolatry. The feeble apprehensions of men cannot be satisfied with conceiving their deity as a pure spirit and perfect intelligence; and yet their natural terrors keep them from imputing to him the least shadow of limitation and imperfection. They fluctuate between these opposite sentiments. The same infirmity still drags them downwards, from an omnipotent and spiritual deity, to a limited and corporeal one, and from a corporeal and limited deity to a statue or visible representation. The same endeavour at elevation still pushes them upwards, from the statue or material image to the invisible power; and from the invisible power to an infinitely perfect deity, the creator and sovereign of the universe.

IX

COMPARISON OF THESE RELIGIONS, WITH REGARD TO PERSECUTION AND TOLERATION

Polytheism or idolatrous worship, being founded entirely in vulgar traditions, is liable to this great inconvenience, that any practice or opinion, however barbarous or corrupted, may be authorized by it; and full scope is given, for knavery to impose on credulity, till morals and humanity be expelled the religious systems of mankind. At the same time, idolatry is attended with this evident advantage, that, by limiting the powers and functions of its deities, it naturally admits the gods of other sects and nations to a share of divinity, and renders all the various deities, as well as rites, ceremonies, or traditions, compatible with each other.[1] Theism is opposite both in its advantages and disadvantages. As that system supposes one sole deity, the perfection of reason and goodness, it should, if justly prosecuted, banish every thing frivolous, unreasonable, or inhuman from religious worship, and set before men the most illustrious example, as well as the most commanding motives, of justice and benevolence. These mighty advantages are not indeed over-balanced (for that is not possible), but somewhat diminished, by inconveniences, which arise from the vices and prejudices of mankind. While one sole object of devotion is acknowledged, the worship of other deities is regarded as absurd and impious. Nay, this unity of object seems naturally to require the unity of faith and ceremonies, and furnishes designing men with a pretence for representing their adversaries as profane, and the objects of divine as well as human vengeance. For as each sect is positive that its own faith and worship are entirely acceptable to the deity, and as no one can conceive, that the same being should be pleased with different and opposite rites and principles; the several sects fall naturally into animosity, and mutually discharge on each other that sacred zeal and rancour, the most furious and implacable of all human passions.

The tolerating spirit of idolaters, both in ancient and modern times, is very obvious to any one, who is the least conversant in the writings of historians or travellers. When the oracle of DELPHI was asked, what rites or worship was most acceptable to the gods? Those which are legally established in each city, replied the oracle.[2] Even priests, in those ages, could, it seems, allow salvation to those of the different communion. The ROMANS commonly adopted the gods of the conquered people; and never disputed the attributes of those local and national deities, in whose territories they resided. The religious wars and persecutions of the EGYPTIAN idolaters are indeed an exception to this

---

[1] VERRIUS FLACCUS, cited by PLINY, lib. xxviii. cap. 2. affirmed, that it was usual for the ROMANS before they laid siege to any town, to invocate the tutelar deity of the place, and by promising him greater honours than those he at present enjoyed, bribe him to betray his old friends and votaries. The name of the tutelar deity of ROME was for this reason kept a most religious mystery; lest the enemies of the republic should be able, in the same manner, to draw him over to their service. For without the name, they thought, nothing of that kind could be practised. PLINY says, that the common form of invocation was preserved to his time in the ritual of the pontiffs. And MACROBIUS has transmitted a copy of it from the secret things of SAMMONICUS SERENUS.

[2] Xenoph. Memor. lib. i. 3, 1.

rule; but are accounted for by ancient authors from reasons singular and remarkable. Different species of animals were the deities of the different sects among the EGYPTIANS; and the deities being in continual war, engaged their votaries in the same contention. The worshippers of dogs could not long remain in peace with the adorers of cats or wolves.[1] But where that reason took not place, the EGYPTIAN superstition was not so incompatible as is commonly imagined; since we learn from HERODOTUS,[2] that very large contributions were given by AMASIS towards rebuilding the temple of DELPHI.

The intolerance of almost all religions, which have maintained the unity of God, is as remarkable as the contrary principle of polytheists. The implacable narrow spirit of the JEWS is well known. MAHOMETANISM set out with still more bloody principles; and even to this day, deals out damnation, though not fire and faggot, to all other sects. And if, among CHRISTIANS, the ENGLISH and DUTCH have embraced the principles of toleration, this singularity has proceeded from the steady resolution of the civil magistrate, in opposition to the continued efforts of priests and bigots.

The disciples of ZOROASTER shut the doors of heaven against all but the MAGIANS.[3] Nothing could more obstruct the progress of the PERSIAN conquests, than the furious zeal of that nation against the temples and images of the GREEKS. And after the overthrow of that empire we find ALEXANDER, as a polytheist, immediately reestablishing the worship of the BABYLONIANS, which their former princes, as monotheists, had carefully abolished.[4] Even the blind and devoted attachment of that conqueror to the GREEK superstition hindered not but he himself sacrificed according to the BABYLONISH rites and ceremonies.[5]

So social is polytheism, that the utmost fierceness and antipathy, which it meets with in an opposite religion, is scarcely able to disgust it, and keep it at a distance. AUGUSTUS praised extremely the reserve of his grandson, CAIUS CÆSAR, when this latter prince, passing by JERUSALEM, deigned not to sacrifice according to the JEWISH law. But for what reason did AUGUSTUS so much approve of this conduct?

1 Plutarch. de Isid. & Osiride. c. 72.
2 Lib. ii. 180.
3 Hyde de Relig. vet. Persarum.
4 Arrian. de Exped, lib. iii. 16. Id. lib. vii. 17.
5 Id. ibid.

Only, because that religion was by the PAGANS esteemed ignoble and barbarous.[1]

I may venture to affirm, that few corruptions of idolatry and polytheism are more pernicious to society than this corruption of theism,[2] when carried to the utmost height. The human sacrifices of the CARTHAGINIANS, MEXICANS, and many barbarous nations,[3] scarcely exceed the inquisition and persecutions of ROME and MADRID. For besides, that the effusion of blood may not be so great in the former case as in the latter; besides this, I say, the human victims, being chosen by lot, or by some exterior signs, affect not, in so considerable a degree, the rest of the society. Whereas virtue, knowledge, love of liberty, are the qualities, that call down the fatal vengeance of inquisitors; and when expelled, leave the society in the most shameful ignorance, corruption, and bondage. The illegal murder of one man by a tyrant is more pernicious than the death of a thousand by pestilence, famine, or any undistinguishing calamity.

In the temple of DIANA at ARICIA near ROME, whoever murdered the present priest, was legally entitled to be installed his successor.[4] A very singular institution! For, however barbarous and bloody the common superstitions often are to the laity, they usually turn to the advantage of the holy order.

X

WITH REGARD TO COURAGE OR ABASEMENT

From the comparison of theism and idolatry, we may form some other observations, which will also confirm the vulgar observation, that the corruption of the best things gives rise to the worst.

[1] Sueton. in vita Aug. c. 93. [2] *Corruptio optimi pessima.*

[3] Most nations have fallen into this guilt of human sacrifices; though, perhaps, this impious superstition has never prevailed very much in any civilized nation, unless we except the CARTHAGINIANS. For the TYRIANS soon abolished it. A sacrifice is conceived as a present; and any present is delivered to their deity by destroying it and rendering it useless to men; by burning what is solid, pouring out the liquid, and killing the animate. For want of a better way of doing him service, we do ourselves an injury; and fancy that we thereby express, at least, the heartiness of our good-will and adoration. Thus our mercenary devotion deceives ourselves, and imagines it deceives the deity.

[4] Strabo, lib. v. 239. Sueton. invita Cal. 35.

Where the deity is represented as infinitely superior to mankind, this belief, though altogether just, is apt, when joined with superstitious terrors, to sink the human mind into the lowest submission and abasement, and to represent the monkish virtues of mortification, penance, humility, and passive suffering, as the only qualities which are acceptable to him. But where the gods are conceived to be only a little superior to mankind, and to have been, many of them, advanced from that inferior rank, we are more at our ease, in our addresses to them, and may even, without profaneness, aspire sometimes to a rivalship and emulation of them. Hence activity, spirit, courage, magnanimity, love of liberty, and all the virtues which aggrandize a people.

The heroes in paganism correspond exactly to the saints in popery, and holy dervises in MAHOMETANISM. The place of HERCULES, THESEUS, HECTOR, ROMULUS, is now supplied by DOMINIC, FRANCIS, ANTHONY, and BENEDICT. Instead of the destruction of monsters, the subduing of tyrants, the defence of our native country; whippings and fastings, cowardice and humility, abject submission and slavish obedience, are become the means of obtaining celestial honours among mankind.

One great incitement to the pious ALEXANDER in his warlike expeditions was his rivalship of HERCULES and BACCHUS, whom he justly pretended to have excelled.[1] BRASIDAS, that generous and noble SPARTAN, after falling in battle, had heroic honours paid him by the inhabitants of AMPHIPOLIS, whose defence he had embraced.[2] And in general, all founders of states and colonies among the GREEKS were raised to this inferior rank of divinity, by those who reaped the benefit of their labours.

This gave rise to the observation of MACHIAVEL,[3] that the doctrines of the CHRISTIAN religion (meaning the catholic; for he knew no other) which recommend only passive courage and suffering, had subdued the spirit of mankind, and had fitted them for slavery and subjection. An observation, which would certainly be just, were there not many other circumstances in human society which controul the genius and character of a religion.

BRASIDAS seized a mouse, and being bit by it, let it go. *There is nothing so contemptible, said he, but what may be safe, if it has but courage*

[1] Arrian passim.   [2] Thucyd. lib. v. 11.
[3] Discorsi. lib. vi.

to defend itself.[1] BELLARMINE patiently and humbly allowed the fleas and other odious vermin to prey upon him. *We shall have heaven,* said he, *to reward us for our sufferings: But these poor creatures have nothing but the enjoyment of the present life.*[2] Such difference is there between the maxims of a GREEK hero and a CATHOLIC saint.

XI

WITH REGARD TO REASON OR ABSURDITY

Here is another observation to the same purpose, and a new proof that the corruption of the best things begets the worst. If we examine, without prejudice, the ancient heathen mythology, as contained in the poets, we shall not discover in it any such monstrous absurdity, as we may at first be apt to apprehend. Where is the difficulty in conceiving, that the same powers or principles, whatever they were, which formed this visible world, men and animals, produced also a species of intelligent creatures, of more refined substance and greater authority than the rest? That these creatures may be capricious, revengeful, passionate, voluptuous, is easily conceived; nor is any circumstance more apt, among ourselves, to engender such vices, than the licence of absolute authority. And in short, the whole mythological system is so natural, that, in the vast variety of planets and world, contained in this universe, it seems more than probable, that, somewhere or other, it is really carried into execution.

The chief objection to it with regard to this planet, is, that it is not ascertained by any just reason or authority. The ancient tradition, insisted on by heathen priests and theologers, is but a weak foundation; and transmitted also such a number of contradictory reports, supported, all of them, by equal authority, that it became absolutely impossible to fix a preference amongst them. A few volumes, therefore, must contain all the polemical writings of pagan priests: And their whole theology must consist more of traditional stories and superstitious practices than of philosophical argument and controversy.

But where theism forms the fundamental principle of any popular religion, that tenet is so conformable to sound reason, that philosophy is apt to incorporate itself with such a system of theology. And if the

[1] Plut. Apopth. [2] Bayle, Article BELLARMINE.

other dogmas of that system be contained in a sacred book, such as the Alcoran, or be determined by any visible authority, like that of the ROMAN pontiff, speculative reasoners naturally carry on their assent, and embrace a theory, which has been instilled into them by their earliest education, and which also possesses some degree of consistence and uniformity. But as these appearances are sure, all of them, to prove deceitful, philosophy will soon find herself very unequally yoked with her new associate; and instead of regulating each principle, as they advance together, she is at every turn perverted to serve the purposes of superstition. For besides the unavoidable incoherences, which must be reconciled and adjusted; one may safely affirm, that all popular theology, especially the scholastic, has a kind of appetite for absurdity and contradiction. If that theology went not beyond reason and common sense, her doctrines would appear too easy and familiar. Amazement must of necessity be raised: Mystery affected: Darkness and obscurity sought after: And a foundation of merit afforded to the devout votaries, who desire an opportunity of subduing their rebellious reason, by the belief of the most unintelligible sophisms.

Ecclesiastical history sufficiently confirms these reflections. When a controversy is started, some people always pretend with certainty to foretell the issue. Whichever opinion, say they, is most contrary to plain sense is sure to prevail; even where the general interest of the system requires not that decision. Though the reproach of heresy may, for some time, be bandied about among the disputants, it always rests at last on the side of reason. Any one, it is pretended, that has but learning enough of this kind to know the definition of ARIAN, PELAGIAN, ERASTIAN, SOCINIAN, SABELLIAN, EUTYCHIAN, NESTORIAN, MONOTHELITE, &c. not to mention PROTESTANT, whose fate is yet uncertain, will be convinced of the truth of this observation. It is thus a system becomes more absurd in the end, merely from its being reasonable and philosophical in the beginning.

To oppose the torrent of scholastic religion by such feeble maxims as these, that *it is impossible for the same thing to be and not to be*, that *the whole is greater than a part,* that *two and three make five*; is pretending to stop the ocean with a bullrush. Will you set up profane reason against sacred mystery? No punishment is great enough for your impiety. And the same fires, which were kindled for heretics, will serve also for the destruction of philosophers.

XII

WITH REGARD TO DOUBT OR CONVICTION

We meet every day with people so sceptical with regard to history, that they assert it impossible for any nation ever to believe such absurd principles as those of GREEK and EGYPTIAN paganism; and at the same time so dogmatical with regard to religion, that they think the same absurdities are to be found in no other communion. CAMBYSES entertained like prejudices; and very impiously ridiculed, and even wounded, APIS, the great god of the EGYPTIANS, who appeared to his profane senses nothing but a large spotted bull. But HERODOTUS judiciously ascribes this sally of passion to a real madness or disorder of the brain: Otherwise, says the historian, he never would have openly affronted any established worship. For on that head, continues he, every nation are best satisfied with their own, and think they have the advantage over every other nation.

It must be allowed, that the ROMAN CATHOLICS are a very learned sect; and that no one communion, but that of the church of ENGLAND, can dispute their being the most learned of all the Christian churches: Yet AVERROES, the famous ARABIAN, who, no doubt, had heard of the EGYPTIAN superstitions, declares, that, of all religions, the most absurd and nonsensical is that, whose votaries eat, after having created, their deity.

I believe, indeed, that there is no tenet in all paganism, which would give so fair a scope to ridicule as this of the *real presence*: For it is so absurd, that it eludes the force of all argument. There are even some pleasant stories of that kind, which, though somewhat profane, are commonly told by the Catholics themselves. One day, a priest, it is said, gave inadvertently, instead of the sacrament, a counter, which had by accident fallen among the holy wafers. The communicant waited patiently for some time, expecting it would dissolve on his tongue: But finding that it still remained entire, he took it off. *I wish*, cried he to the priest, *you have not committed some mistake: I wish you have not given me God the Father: He is so hard and tough there is no swallowing him.*

A famous general, at that time in the MUSCOVITE service, having come to PARIS for the recovery of his wounds, brought along with him a young TURK, whom he had taken prisoner. Some of the doctors of the SORBONNE (who are altogether as positive as the dervishes of CONSTANTINOPLE) thinking it a pity, that the poor TURK should be damned for want of instruction, solicited MUSTAPHA very hard to turn Christian, and promised him, for his encouragement, plenty of good wine in this world, and paradise in the next. These allurements were too powerful to be resisted; and therefore, having been well instructed and catechized, he at last agreed to receive the sacraments of baptism and the Lord's supper. The priest, however, to make every thing sure and solid, still continued his instructions, and began the next day with the usual question, *How many Gods are there? None at all,* replies BENEDICT; for that was his new name. *How! None at all!* cries the priest. *To be sure,* said the honest proselyte. *You have told me all along that there is but one God: And yesterday I eat him.*

Such are the doctrines of our brethren the Catholics. But to these doctrines we are so accustomed, that we never wonder at them: Though in a future age, it will probably become difficult to persuade some nations, that any human, two-legged creature could ever embrace such principles. And it is a thousand to one, but these nations themselves shall have something full as absurd in their own creed, to which they will give a most implicit and most religious assent.

I lodged once at PARIS in the same *hotel* with an ambassador from TUNIS, who, having passed some years at LONDON, was returning home that way. One day I observed his MOORISH excellency diverting himself under the porch, with surveying the splendid equipages that drove along; when there chanced to pass that way some *Capucin* friars, who had never seen a TURK; as he, on his part, though accustomed to the EUROPEAN dresses, had never seen the grotesque figure of a *Capucin*: And there is no expressing the mutual admiration, with which they inspired each other. Had the chaplain of the embassy entered into a dispute with these FRANCISCANS, their reciprocal surprize had been of the same nature. Thus all mankind stand staring at one another; and there is no beating it into their heads, that the turban of the AFRICAN is not just as good or as bad a fashion as the cowl of the EUROPEAN. *He is a very honest man,* said the prince of SALLEE, speaking of DE RUYTER. *It is a pity he were a Christian.*

How can you worship leeks and onions? we shall suppose a SORBONNIST to say to a priest of SAIS. If we worship them, replies the latter; at least, we do not, at the same time, eat them. But what strange objects or adoration are cats and monkeys? says the learned doctor. They are at least as good as the relics or rotten bones of martyrs, answers his no less learned antagonist. Are you not mad, insists the Catholic, to cut one another's throat about the preference of a cabbage or a cucumber? Yes, says the pagan; I allow it, if you will confess, that those are still madder, who fight about the preference among volumes of sophistry, ten thousand of which are not equal in value to one cabbage or cucumber.[1]

Every by-stander will easily judge (but unfortunately the bystanders are few) that, if nothing were requisite to establish any popular system, but exposing the absurdities of other systems, every voter of every superstition could give a sufficient reason for his blind and bigotted attachment to the principles in which he has been educated. But without so extensive a knowledge, on which to ground this assurance (and perhaps, better without it), there is not wanting a sufficient stock of religious zeal and faith among mankind. DIODORUS SICULUS[2] gives a remarkable instance to this purpose, of which he was himself an eye-witness While EGYPT lay under the greatest terror of the ROMAN name, a legionary soldier having inadvertently been guilty of the sacrilegious impiety of killing a cat, the whole people rose upon him with the utmost fury; and all the efforts of the prince were not able to save him. The senate and people of ROME, I am persuaded, would not, then, have been so delicate with regard to their national deities.

---

[1] It is strange that the EGYPTIAN religion, though so absurd, should yet have borne so great a resemblance to the JEWISH that ancient writers, even of the greatest genius were not able to observe any difference between them. For it is very remarkable that both TACITUS and SUETONIUS, when they mention that decree of the senate, under TIBERIUS, by which the EGYPTIAN and JEWISH proselytes were banished from ROME, expressly treat these religions as the same; and it appears, that even the decree itself was founded on that supposition. 'Actum & de sacris ÆGYPTIIS JUDAICISQUE pellendis; factumque patrum consultum, ut quatuor millia libertini generis ea superstitione infecta, quis idonea ætas, in insulam Sardiniam veherentur, coercendis illic latrociniis; & si ob gravitatem cœli interissent, vile damnum: Ceteri cederent ITALIA, nisi certam ante diem profanos ritus exuissent.' TACIT. ann. lib. ii. c. 85. 'Externas cæremonias, ÆGYPTIOS JUDAICOSQUE ritus compescuit; coactis qui superstitione ea tenebantur, religiosas vestes cum instruento omni comburere, &c.' SUETON. TIBER. c. 36. These wise heathens, observing something in the general air, and genius, and spirit of the two religions to be the same, esteemed the difference of their dogmas too frivolous to deserve any attention.

[2] Lib. i. 83.

They very frankly, a little after that time, voted AUGUSTUS a place in the celestial mansions; and would have dethroned every god in heaven, for his sake, had he seemed to desire it. *Presens divus habebitur* AUGUSTUS, says HORACE. That is a very important point: And in other nations and other ages, the same circumstance has not been deemed altogether indifferent.[1]

Notwithstanding the sanctity of our holy religion, says TULLY,[2] no crime is more common with us than sacrilege: But was it ever heard of, that an EGYPTIAN violated the temple of a cat, an ibis, or a crocodile? There is no torture, an EGYPTIAN would not undergo, says the same author in another place,[3] rather than injure an ibis, an aspic, a cat, a dog, or a crocodile. Thus it is strictly true, what DRYDEN observes,

> ' Of whatsoe'er descent their godhead be,
> ' Stock, stone, or other homely pedigree,
> ' In his defence his servants are as bold
> ' As if he had been born of beaten gold.'
>
> ABSALOM and ACHITOPHEL

Nay, the baser the materials are, of which the divinity is composed, the greater devotion is he likely to excite in the breasts of his deluded votaries. They exult in their shame and make a merit with their deity, in braving, for his sake, all the ridicule and contumely of his enemies. Ten thousand Crusaders inlist themselves under the holy banners; and even openly triumph in those parts of their religion, which their adversaries regard as the most reproachful.

There occurs, I own, a difficulty in the EGYPTIAN system of theology; as indeed, few systems of that kind are entirely free from difficulties. It is evident, from their method of propagation, that a couple of cats, in fifty years, would stock a whole kingdom; and if that religious veneration were still paid them, it would, in twenty more,

---

1 When LOUIS the XIVth took on himself the protection of the Jesuit's College of CLERMONT, the society ordered the king's arms to be put up over the gate, and took down the cross in order to make way for it: Which gave occasion to the following epigram:

> Sustulit hinc Christi, posuitque insignia Regis:
> Impia gens, alium nescit habere Deum.

2 De nat. Deor. i. 29.
3 Tusc. Quæst. lib. v. 27.

not only be easier in EGYPT to find a god than a man, which PETRON-
IUS says was the case in some parts of Italy; but the gods must at last
entirely starve the men, and leave themselves neither priests nor
votaries remaining. It is probable, therefore, that this wise nation,
the most celebrated in antiquity for prudence and sound policy, fore-
seeing such dangerous consequences, reserved all their worship for
the full-grown divinities, and used the freedom to drown the holy
spawn or little sucking gods, without any scruple or remorse. And thus
the practice of warping the tenets of religion, in order to serve temporal
interests, is not, by any means, to be regarded as an invention of these
later ages.

The learned, philosophical VARRO, discoursing of religion, pretends
not to deliver any thing beyond probabilities and appearances: Such
was his good sense and moderation! But the passionate, the zealous
AUGUSTIN, insults the noble ROMAN on his scepticism and reserve,
and professes the most thorough belief and assurance.[1] A heathen poet,
however, contemporary with the saint, absurdly esteems the religious
system of the latter so false, that even the credulity of children, he says,
could not engage to believe it.[2]

It is strange, when mistakes are so common, to find every one
positive and dogmatical? And that the zeal often rises in proportion to
the error? *Moverunt*, says SPARTIAN, *& ca tempestate, Judæi bellum quod
vetabantur mutilare genitalia.*[3]

If ever there was a nation or a time, in which the public religion lost
all authority over mankind, we might expect, that infidelity in ROME,
during the CICERONIAN age, would openly have erected its throne,
and that CICERO himself, in every speech and action, would have
been its most declared abettor. But it appears, that, whatever sceptical
liberties that great man might take, in his writings or in philosophical
conversation; he yet avoided, in the common conduct of life, the
imputation of deism and profaneness. Even in his own family, and to
his wife TERENTIA, whom he highly trusted, he was willing to appear
a devout religionist; and there remains a letter, addressed to her, in
which he seriously desires her to offer sacrifice to APOLLO and
ÆSCULAPIUS, in gratitude for the recovery of his health.[4]

[1] De civitate Dei, l. iii. c. 17.
[2] Claudii Rutilii Numitiani iter, lib. i. l. 394.
[3] In vita Adriani. 14. [4] Lib. xiv. epist. 7.

POMPEY'S devotion was much more sincere: In all his conduct, during the civil wars, he paid a great regard to auguries, dreams, and prophesies.[1] AUGUSTUS was tainted with superstition of every kind. As it is reported of MILTON, that his poetical genius never flowed with ease and abundance in the spring; so AUGUSTUS observed, that his own genius for dreaming never was so perfect during that season, nor was so much to be relied on, as during the rest of the year. That great and able emperor was also extremely uneasy, when he happened to change his shoes, and put the right foot shoe on the left foot.[2] In short it cannot be doubted, but the votaries of the established superstition of antiquity were as numerous in every state, as those of the modern religion are at present. Its influence was as universal; though it was not so great. As many people gave their assent to it; though that assent was not seemingly so strong, precise, and affirmative.

We may observe, that, notwithstanding the dogmatical, imperious style of all superstition, the conviction of the religionists, in all ages, is more affected than real, and scarcely ever approaches, in any degree, to that solid belief and persuasion, which governs us in the common affairs of life. Men dare not avow, even to their own hearts, the doubts which they entertain on such subjects: They make a merit of implicit faith; and disguise to themselves their real infidelity, by the strongest asseverations and most positive bigotry. But nature is too hard for all their endeavours, and suffers not the obscure, glimmering light, afforded in those shadowy regions, to equal the strong impressions, made by common sense and by experience. The usual course of men's conduct belies their words, and shows, that their assent in these matters is some unaccountable operation of the mind between disbelief and conviction, but approaching much nearer to the former than to the latter.

Since, therefore, the mind of man appears of so loose and unsteady a texture, that, even at present, when so many persons find an interest in continually employing on it the chissel and the hammer, yet are they not able to engrave theological tenets with any lasting impression; how much more must this have been the case in ancient times, when the retainers to the holy function were so much fewer in comparison? No wonder, that the appearances were then very inconsistent, and that

[1] Cicero de Divin. lib. ii. c. 24.
[2] Sueton. Aug. cap. 90, 91, 92. Plin. lib. ii. cap. 5.

men, on some occasions, might seem determined infidels, and enemies to the established religion, without being so in reality; or at least, without knowing their own minds in that particular.

Another cause, which rendered the ancient religion much looser than the modern, is, that the former were *traditional* and the latter are *scriptural*; and the tradition in the former was complex, contradictory, and, on many occasions, doubtful; so that it could not possibly be reduced to any standard and canon, or afford any determinate articles of faith. The stories of the gods were numberless like the popish legends; and though every one, almost, believed a part of these stories, yet no one could believe or know the whole: While, at the same time, all must have acknowledged, that no one part stood on a better foundation than the rest. The traditions of different cities and nations were also, on many occasions, directly opposite; and no reason could be assigned for preferring one to the other. And as there was an infinite number of stories, with regard to which tradition was nowise positive; the gradation was insensible, from the most fundamental articles of faith, to those loose and precarious fictions. The pagan religion, therefore, seemed to vanish like a cloud, whenever one approached to it, and examined it piecemeal. It could never be ascertained by any fixed dogmas and principles. And though this did not convert the generality of mankind from so absurd a faith; for when will the people be reasonable? yet it made them faulter and hesitate more in maintaining their principles, and was even apt to produce, in certain dispositions of mind, some practices and opinions, which had the appearance of determined infidelity.

To which we may add, that the fables of the pagan religion were, of themselves, light, easy, and familiar; without devils, or seas of brimstone, or any object that could much terrify the imagination. Who could forbear smiling, when he thought of the loves of MARS and VENUS, or the amorous frolics of JUPITER and PAN? In this respect, it was a true poetical religion; if it had not rather too much levity for the graver kinds of poetry. We find that it has been adopted by modern bards; nor have these talked with greater freedom and irreverence of the gods, whom they regarded as fictions, than the ancients did of the real objects of their devotion.

The inference is by no means just, that, because a system of religion has made no deep impression on the minds of a people, it must therefore have been positively rejected by all men of common sense, and that opposite principles, in spite of the prejudices of education, were generally established by argument and reasoning. I know not, but a contrary inference may be more probable. The less importunate and assuming any species of superstition appears, the less will it provoke men's spleen and indignation, or engage them into enquiries concerning its foundation and origin. This in the mean time is obvious, that the empire of all religious faith over the understanding is wavering and uncertain, subject to every variety of humour, and dependent on the present incidents, which strike the imagination. The difference is only in the degrees. An ancient will place a stroke of impiety and one of superstition alternately, throughout a whole discourse;[1] A modern often thinks in the same way, though he may be more guarded in his expression.

LUCIAN tells us expressly,[2] that whoever believed not the most ridiculous fables of paganism was deemed by the people profane and impious. To what purpose, indeed, would that agreeable author have employed the whole force of his wit and satire against the national religion, had not that religion been generally believed by his country-men and contemporaries?

LIVY[3] acknowledges as frankly, as any divine would at present, the common incredulity of his age; but then he condemns it as severely. And who can imagine, that a national superstition, which could delude so ingenious a man, would not also impose on the generality of the people?

The STOICS bestowed many magnificent and even impious epithets on their sage; that he alone was rich, free, a king, and equal to the immortal gods. They forgot to add, that he was not inferior in prudence and understanding to an old woman. For surely nothing can be more

---

[1] Witness this remarkable passage of TACITUS: 'Præter multiplices rerum humanarum casus cœlo terraque prodigia & fulminum monitus & futurorum præsagia, læta tristia, ambigua manifesta. Nec enim unquam atrocioribus populi Romani cladibus, magisve justis indiciis approbatum est, non esse curæ Diis securitatem nostram, esse ultionem.' Hist. lib. i. 3. AUGUSTUS's quarrel with NEPTUNE is an instance of the same kind. Had not the emperor believed NEPTUNE to be a real being, and to have dominion over the sea, where had been the foundation of his anger? And if he believed it, what madness to provoke still farther that deity? The same observation may be made upon QUINTILIAN's exclamation, on account of the death of his children, lib. vi. Præf.
[2] Philopseudes. 3.   [3] Lib. x. cap. 40.

pitiful than the sentiments, which that sect entertain with regard to religious matters; while they seriously agree with the common augurs, that, when a raven croaks from the left, it is a good omen; but a bad one, when a rook makes a noise from the same quarter. PANÆTIUS was the only STOIC, among the GREEKS, who so much as doubted with regard to auguries and divination.[1] MARCUS ANTONINUS[2] tells us, that he himself had received many admonitions from the gods in his sleep. It is true, EPICTETUS[3] forbids us to regard the language of rooks and ravens; but it is not, that they do not speak truth: It is only, because they can fortel nothing but the breaking of our neck or the forfeiture of our estate; which are circumstances, says he, that nowise concern us. Thus the STOICS join a philosophical enthusiasm to a religious superstition. The force of their mind, being all turned to the side of morals, unbent itself in that of religion.[4]

PLATO[5] introduces SOCRATES affirming, that the accusation of impiety raised against him was owing entirely to his rejecting such fables, as those of SATURN's castrating his father URANUS, and JUPITER's dethroning SATURN: Yet in a subsequent dialogue,[6] SOCRATES confesses, that the doctrine of the mortality of the soul was the received opinion of the people. Is there here any contradiction? Yes, surely: But the contradiction is not in PLATO; it is in the people, whose religious principles in general are always composed of the most discordant parts; especially in an age, when superstition sate so easy and light upon them.[7]

---

1 Cicero de Divin. lib. i. cap. 3 & 7.
2 Lib. i. § 17.   3 Ench. § 17.
4 The Stoics, I own, were not quite orthodox in the established religion; but one may see, from these instances, that they went a great way: And the people undoubtedly went every length.
5 Euthyphro. 6.   6 Phædo.
7 XENOPHON's conduct, as related by himself, is, at once, an incontestable proof of the general credulity of mankind in those ages, and the incoherencies, in all ages, of men's opinions in religious matters. That great captain and philosopher, the disciple of SOCRATES, and one who has delivered some of the most refined sentiments with regard to a deity, gave all the following marks of vulgar, pagan superstition. By SOCRATES's advice, he consulted the oracle of DELPHI, before he would engage in the expedition of CYRUS. De exped. lib. iii. p. 294, ex edit. Leuncl. Sees a dream the night after the generals were seized; which he pays great regard to, but thinks ambiguous. Id. p. 295. He and the whole army regard sneezing as a very lucky omen. Id. p. 300. Has another dream, when he comes to the river CENTRITES, which his fellow-general, CHIROSPHUS, also pays great regard to. Id. lib. iv. p. 323. The GREEKS, suffering from a cold north

The same CICERO, who affected, in his own family, to appear a devout religionist, makes no scruple, in a public court of judicature, of treating the doctrine of a future state as a ridiculous fable, to which no body could give any attention.[1] SALLUST[2] represents CÆSAR as speaking the same language in the open senate.[3]

But that all these freedoms implied not a total and universal infidelity and scepticism amongst the people, is too apparent to be denied. Though some parts of the national religion hung loose upon the minds of men, other parts adhered more closely to them: And it was the chief business of the sceptical philosophers to show, that there was no more foundation for one than for the other. This is the artifice of COTTA in the dialogues concerning the *nature of the gods*. He refutes the

wind, sacrifice to it; and the historian observes, that it immediately abated. Id. p. 329. XENOPHON consults the sacrifices in secret, before he would form any resolution with himself about settling a colony. Lib. v. p. 359. He was himself a very skilful augur. Id. p. 361. Is determined by the victims to refuse the sole command of the army which was offered him. Lib. vi. p. 273. CLEANDER, the SPARTAN, though very desirous of it, refuses for the same reason. Id. p. 392. XENOPHON, mentions an old dream with the interpretation given him, when he first joined CYRUS, p. 373. Mentions also the place of HERCULES's descent into hell as believing it, and says the marks of it are still remaining. Id. p. 375. Had almost starved the army, rather than lead them to the field against the auspices. Id. p. 382, 383. His friend, EUCLIDES, the augur, would not believe that he had brought no money from the expedition; till he (EUCLIDES) sacrificed, and then he saw the matter clearly in the Exta. Lib. vii. p. 425. The same philosopher, proposing a project of mines for the encrease of the ATHENIAN revenues, advises them first to consult the oracle. De rat. red. p. 392. That all this devotion was not a farce, in order to serve a political purpose, appears both from the facts themselves, and from the genius of that age, when little or nothing could be gained by hypocrisy. Besides, XENOPHON, as appears from his Memorabilia, was a kind of heretic in those times, which no political devotee ever is. It is for the same reason, I maintain, that NEWTON, LOCKE, CLARKE, &c. being *Arians* or *Socinians*, were very sincere in the creed they professed: And I always oppose this argument to some libertines, who will needs have it, that it was impossible but that these philosophers must have been hypocrites.

[1] PRO CLUENTIO, cap. 61.

[2] De bello CATILIN. 51.

[3] CICERO (Tusc. Quæst. lib. i. cap. 5, 6) and SENECA (Epist. 24) as also JUVENAL (Satyr. 2. 149), maintain that there is no boy or old woman so ridiculous as to believe the poets in their accounts of a future state. Why then does LUCRETIUS so highly exalt his master for freeing us from these terrors? Perhaps the generality of mankind were then in the disposition of CEPHALUS in PLATO (de Rep. lib. i. 330 D.) who while he was young and healthful could ridicule these stories; but as soon as he became old and infirm, began to entertain apprehensions of their truth. This we may observe not to be unusual even at present.

whole system of mythology by leading the orthodox gradually, from the more momentous stories, which were believed, to the more frivolous, which every one ridiculed: From the gods to the goddesses; from the goddesses to the nymphs; from the nymphs to the fawns and satyrs. His master, CARNEADES, had employed the same method of reasoning.[1]

Upon the whole, the greatest and most observable differences between a *traditional, mythological* religion, and a *systematical, scholastic* one are two: The former is often more reasonable, as consisting only of a multitude of stories, which, however groundless, imply no express absurdity and demonstrative contradiction; and sits also so easy and light on men's minds, that, though it may be as universally received, it happily makes no such deep impression on the affections and understanding.

XIII

IMPIOUS CONCEPTIONS OF THE DIVINE NATURE IN POPULAR RELIGIONS OF BOTH KINDS

The primary religion of mankind arises chiefly from an anxious fear of future events; and what ideas will naturally be entertained of invisible, unknown powers, while men lie under dismal apprehensions of any kind, may easily be conceived. Every image of vengeance, severity, cruelty, and malice must occur, and must augment the ghastliness and horror, which oppresses the amazed religionist. A panic having once seized the mind, the active fancy still farther multiplies the objects of terror; while that profound darkness, or, what is worse, that glimmering light, with which we are environed, represents the spectres of divinity under the most dreadful appearances imaginable. And no idea of perverse wickedness can be framed, which those terrified devotees do not readily, without scruple, apply to their deity.

This appears the natural state of religion, when surveyed in one light. But if we consider, on the other hand, that spirit of praise and eulogy, which necessarily has place in all religions, and which is the

[1] SEXT. EMPIR. advers. MATHEM. lib. ix. 429.

consequence of these very terrors, we must expect a quite contrary system of theology to prevail. Every virtue, every excellence, must be ascribed to the divinity, and no exaggeration will be deemed sufficient to reach those perfections, with which he is endowed. Whatever strains of panegyric can be invented, are immediately embraced, without consulting any arguments of phænomena: It is esteemed a sufficient confirmation of them, that they give us more magnificent ideas of the divine objects of our worship and adoration.

Here therefore is a kind of contradiction between the different principles of human nature, which enter into religion. Our natural terrors present the notion of a devilish and malicious deity: Our propensity to adulation leads us to acknowledge an excellent and divine. And the influence of these opposite principles are various, according to the different situation of the human understanding.

In very barbarous and ignorant nations, such as the AFRICANS and INDIANS, nay even the JAPONESE, who can form no extensive ideas of power and knowledge, worship may be paid to a being, whom they confess to be wicked and detestable; though they may be cautious, perhaps, of pronouncing this judgment of him in public, or in his temple, where he may be supposed to hear their reproaches.

Such rude, imperfect ideas of the Divinity adhere long to all idolaters; and it may safely be affirmed, that the GREEKS themselves never got entirely rid of them. It is remarked by XENOPHON,[1] in praise of SOCRATES, that this philosopher assented not to the vulgar opinion, which supposed the gods to know some things, and be ignorant of others: He maintained, that they knew every thing; what was done, said, or even thought. But as this was a train of philosophy[2] much above the conception of his countrymen, we need not be surprised, if very frankly, in their books and conversation, they blamed the deities, whom they worshipped in their temples. It is observable, that HERODOTUS in particular scruples not, in many passages, to ascribe *envy* to the gods; a sentiment, of all others, the most suitable to a mean and devilish nature. The pagan hymns, however, sung in public worship, contained nothing but epithets of praise; even while the actions

---

[1] Mem. lib. i l, 19.
[2] It was considered among the ancients, as a very extraordinary, philosophical paradox, that the presence of the gods was not confined to the heavens, but was extended every where; as we learn from LUCIAN. *Hermotimus sive De sectis,* 81.

ascribed to the gods were the most barbarous and detestable. When TIMOTHEUS, the poet, recited a hymn to DIANA, in which he enumerated, with the greatest eulogies, all the actions and attributes of that cruel, capricious goddess: *May your daughter*, said one present, *become such as the deity whom you celebrate.*[1]

But as men farther exalt their idea of their divinity; it is their notion of his power and knowledge only, not of his goodness, which is improved. On the contrary, in proportion to the supposed extent of his science and authority, their terrors naturally augment; while they believe, that no secrecy can conceal them from his scrutiny, and that even the inmost recesses of their breast lie open before him. They must then be careful not to form expressly any sentiment of blame and disapprobation. All must be applause, ravishment, extacy. And while their gloomy apprehensions make them ascribe to him measures of conduct, which, in human creatures, would be highly blamed, they must still affect to praise and admire that conduct in the object of their devotional addresses. Thus it may safely be affirmed, that popular religions are really, in the conception of their more vulgar votaries, a species of dæmonism; and the higher the deity is exalted in power and knowledge, the lower of course is he depressed in goodness and benevolence; whatever epithets of praise may be bestowed on him by his amazed adorers. Among idolaters, the words may be false, and belie the secret opinion: But among more exalted religionists, the opinion itself contracts a kind of falsehood, and belies the inward sentiment. The heart secretly detests such measures of cruel and implacable vengeance; but the judgment dares not but pronounce them perfect and adorable. And the additional misery of this inward struggle aggravates all the other terrors, by which these unhappy victims to superstition are for ever haunted.

LUCIAN[2] observes that a young man, who reads the history of the gods in HOMER or HESIOD, and finds their factions, wars, injustice, incest, adultery, and other immoralities so highly celebrated, is much surprised afterwards, when he comes into the world, to observe that punishments are by law inflicted on the same actions, which he had been taught to ascribe to superior beings. The contradiction is still perhaps stronger between the representations given us by some later religions and our natural ideas of generosity, lenity, impartiality, and

---

[1] PLUTARCH, de Superstit. 10.   [2] Necyomantia, 3.

justice; and in proportion to the multiplied terrors of these religions, the barbarous conceptions of the divinity are multiplied upon us.[1] Nothing can preserve untainted the genuine principles of morals in our judgment of human conduct, but the absolute necessity of these principles to the existence of society. If common conception can

1 Bacchus, a divine being, is represented by the heathen mythology as the inventor of dancing and the theatre. Plays were anciently even a part of public worship on the most solemn occasions, and often employed in times of pestilence, to appease the offended deities. But they have been zealously proscribed by the godly in later ages; and the playhouse, according to a learned divine, is the porch of hell.

But in order to show more evidently, that it is possible for a religion to represent the divinity in still a more immoral and unamiable light than he was pictured by the ancients, we shall cite a long passage from an author of taste and imagination, who was surely no enemy to Christianity. It is the Chevalier R A M S A Y, a writer, who had so laudable an inclination to be orthodox, that his reason never found any difficulty, even in the doctrines which free-thinkers scruple the most, the trinity, incarnation, and satisfaction: His humanity alone, of which he seems to have had a great stock, rebelled against the doctrines of eternal reprobation and predestination. He expresses himself thus: 'What strange ideas,' says he, 'would an Indian or a Chinese philosopher have of our holy religion, if they judged by the schemes given of it by our modern free-thinkers, and pharisaical doctors of all sects? According to the odious and too *vulgar* system of these incredulous scoffers and credulous scribblers, "The God of the Jews is a most cruel, unjust, partial, and fantastical being. He created, about 6000 years ago, a man and a woman, and placed them in a fine garden of A S I A, of which there are no remains. This garden was furnished with all sorts of trees, fountains, and flowers. He allowed them the use of all the fruits of this beautiful garden, except one, that was planted in the midst thereof, and that had in it a secret virtue of preserving them in continual health and vigour of body and mind, of exalting their natural powers and making them wise. The devil entered into the body of a serpent, and solicited the first woman to eat of this forbidden fruit; she engaged her husband to do the same. To punish this slight curiosity and natural desire of life and knowledge, God not only threw our first parents out of paradise, but he condemned all their posterity to temporal misery, and the greatest part of them to eternal pains, though the souls of these innocent children have no more relation to that of A D A M than to those of N E R O and M A H O M E T ; since, according to the scholastic drivellers, fabulists, and mythologists, all souls are created pure, and infused immediately into mortal bodies, as soon as the fœtus is formed. To accomplish the barbarous, partial decree of predestination and reprobation, God abandoned all nations to darkness, idolatry, and superstition, without any saving knowledge or salutary graces; unless it was one particular nation, whom he chose as his peculiar people. This chosen nation was, however, the most stupid, ungrateful, rebellious and perfidious of all nations. After God had thus kept the far greater part of all the human species, during near 4000 years, in a reprobate state, he changed all of a sudden, and took a fancy for other nations besides the J E W S. Then he sent his only begotten Son to the world, under a human form, to appease his wrath, satisfy his vindictive justice, and die for the pardon of sin.

indulge princes in a system of ethics, somewhat different from that which should regulate private persons; how much more those superior beings, whose attributes, views, and nature are so totally unknown to us? *Sunt superis sua jura.*[1] The gods have maxims of justice peculiar to themselves.

Very few nations, however, have heard of this gospel; and all the rest, though left in invincible ignorance, are damned without exception, or any possibility of remission. The greatest part of those who have heard of it, have changed only some speculative notions about God, and some external forms in worship: For, in other respects, the bulk of Christians have continued as corrupt as the rest of mankind in their morals; yea, so much the more perverse and criminal, that their lights were greater. Unless it be a very small select number, all other Christians, like the pagans, will be for ever damned; the great sacrifice offered up for them will become void and of no effect; God will take delight for ever, in their torments and blasphemies; and though he can, by one *fiat* change their hearts, yet they will remain, for ever unconverted and unconvertible, because he will be for ever unappeasable and irreconcileable. It is true, that all this makes God odious, a hater of souls, rather than a lover of them; a cruel, vindictive tyrant, an impotent or a wrathful dæmon, rather than an all-powerful, beneficent father of spirits: Yet all this is a mystery. He has secret reasons for his conduct, that are impenetrable; and though he appears unjust and barbarous, yet we must believe the contrary, because what is injustice, crime, cruelty, and the blackest malice in us, is in him justice, mercy, and sovereign goodness." Thus the incredulous free-thinkers, the judaizing Christians, and the fatalistic doctors have disfigured and dishonoured the sublime mysteries of our holy faith; thus they have confounded the nature of good and evil; transformed the most monstrous passions into divine attributes, and surpassed the pagans in blasphemy, by ascribing to the eternal nature, as perfections, what makes the most horrid crimes amongst men. The grosser pagans contented themselves with divinizing lust, incest, and adultery; but the predestinarian doctors have divinized cruelty, wrath, fury, vengeance and all the blackest vices.' See the Chevalier R AMSAY's philosophical principles of natural and revealed religion, Part ii. p. 401.

The same author asserts, in other places, that the *Arminian* and *Molinist* schemes serve very little to mend the matter: And having thus thrown himself out of all received sects of Christianity, he is obliged to advance a system of his own, which is a kind of *Origenism*, and supposes the pre-existence of the souls both of men and beasts, and the eternal salvation and conversion of all men, beasts, and devils. But this notion, being quite peculiar to himself, we need not treat of. I thought the opinions of this ingenious author very curious; but I pretend not to warrant the justice of them.

[1] OVID. Metam. lib. ix. 499.

XIV

BAD INFLUENCE OF POPULAR RELIGIONS ON MORALITY

Here I cannot forbear observing a fact, which may be worth the attention of such as make human nature the object of their enquiry. It is certain, that, in every religion, however sublime the verbal definition which it gives of its divinity, many of the votaries, perhaps the greatest number, will still seek the divine favour, not by virtue and good morals, which alone can be acceptable to a perfect being, but either by frivolous observances, by intemperate zeal, by rapturous extasies, or by the belief of mysterious and absurd opinions. The least part of the *Sadder*, as well as of the *Pentateuch*, consists in precepts of morality; and we may also be assured, that that part was always the least observed and regarded. When the old ROMANS were attacked with a pestilence, they never ascribed their sufferings to their vices, or dreamed of repentance and amendment. They never thought, that they were the general robbers of the world, whose ambition and avarice made desolate the earth, and reduced opulent nations to want and beggary. They only created a dictator,[1] in order to drive a nail into a door; and by that means, they thought that they had sufficiently appeased their incensed deity.

In ÆGINA, one faction forming a conspiracy, barbarously and treacherously assassinated seven hundred of their fellow-citizens; and carried their fury so far, that, one miserable fugitive having fled to the temple, they cut off his hands, by which he clung to the gates, and carrying him out of holy ground, immediately murdered him. *By this impiety*, says HERODOTUS,[2] (not by the other many cruel assassinations) *they offended the gods, and contracted an inexpiable guilt.*

Nay, if we should suppose, what never happens, that a popular religion were found, in which it was expressly declared, that nothing but morality could gain the divine favour; if an order of priests were instituted to inculcate this opinion, in daily sermons, and with all the arts of persuasion; yet so inveterate are the people's prejudices, that,

1 Called Dictator clavis figendæ causa. T. LIVII. l. vii. c. 3.
2 Lib. vi. 91.

for want of some other superstition, they would make the very attendance on these sermons the essentials of religion, rather than place them in virtue and good morals. The sublime prologue of ZALEU-CUS's laws[1] inspired not the LOCRIANS, so far as we can learn, with any sounder notions of the measures of acceptance with the deity, than were familiar to the other GREEKS.

This observation, then, holds universally: But still one may be at some loss to account for it. It is not sufficient to observe, that the people, every where, degrade their deities into a similitude with themselves, and consider them merely as a species of human creatures, somewhat more potent and intelligent. This will not remove the difficulty. For there is no *man* so stupid, as that, judging by his natural reason, he would not esteem virtue and honesty the most valuable qualities, which any person could possess. Why not ascribe the same sentiment to his deity? Why not make all religion, or the chief part of it, to consist in these attainments?

Nor is it satisfactory to say, that the practice of morality is more difficult than that of superstition; and is therefore rejected. For, not to mention the excessive penances of the *Brachmans* and *Talapoins*; it is certain, that the *Rhamadan* of the TURKS, during which the poor wretches, for many days, often in the hottest months of the year, and in some of the hottest climates of the world, remain without eating or drinking from the rising to the setting sun; this *Rhamadan*, I say, must be more severe than the practice of any moral duty, even to the most vicious and depraved of mankind. The four lents of the MUSCOVITES, and the austerities of some *Roman Catholics*, appear more disagreeable than meekness and benevolence. In short, all virtue, when men are reconciled to it by ever so little practice, is agreeable: All superstition is for ever odious and burthensome.

Perhaps, the following account may be received as a true solution of the difficulty. The duties, which a man performs as a friend or parent, seem merely owing to his benefactor or children; nor can he be wanting to these duties, without breaking through all the ties of nature and morality. A strong inclination may prompt him to the performance: A sentiment of order and moral obligation joins its force to these natural ties: And the whole man, if truly virtuous, is drawn to his duty, without any effort or endeavour. Even with regard to the virtues, which are

[1] To be found in DIOD. SIC. lib. xii. 120.

more austere, and more founded on reflection, such as public spirit, filial duty, temperance, or integrity; the moral obligation, in our apprehension, removes all pretension to religious merit; and the virtuous conduct is deemed no more than what we owe to society and to ourselves. In all this, a superstitious man finds nothing, which he has properly performed for the sake of his deity, or which can peculiarly recommend him to the divine favour and protection. He considers not, that the most genuine method of serving the divinity is by promoting the happiness of his creatures. He still looks out for some more immediate service of the supreme Being, in order to allay those terrors, with which he is haunted. And any practice, recommended to him, which either serves to no purpose in life, or offers the strongest violence to his natural inclinations; that practice he will the more readily embrace, on account of those very circumstances, which should make him absolutely reject it. It seems the more purely religious, because it proceeds from no mixture of any other motive or consideration. And if, for its sake, he sacrifices much of his ease and quiet, his claim of merit appears still to rise upon him, in proportion to the zeal and devotion which he discovers. In restoring a loan, or paying a debt, his divinity is nowise beholden to him; because these acts of justice are what he was bound to perform, and what many would have performed, were there no god in the universe. But if he fast a day, or give himself a sound whipping; this has a direct reference, in his opinion, to the service of God. No other motive could engage him to such austerities. By these distinguished marks of devotion, he has now acquired the divine favour; and may expect, in recompense, protection and safety in this world, and eternal happiness in the next.

Hence the greatest crimes have been found, in many instances, compatible with a superstitious piety and devotion; Hence, it is justly regarded as unsafe to draw any certain inference in favour of a man's morals, from the fervour or strictness of his religious exercises, even though he himself believe them sincere. Nay, it has been observed, that enormities of the blackest dye have been rather apt to produce superstitious terrors, and encrease the religious passion. BOMILCAR, having formed a conspiracy for assassinating at once the whole senate of CARTHAGE, and invading the liberties of his country, lost the opportunity, from a continual regard to omens and prophecies. *Those who undertake the most criminal and most dangerous enterprizes are commonly the most superstitious*; as an ancient historian[1] remarks on this occasion. Their devotion and spiritual faith rise with their fears. CATILINE was not contented with the established deities and received rites of the national religion: His anxious terrors made him seek new inventions of this kind;[2] which he never probably had dreamed of, had he remained a good citizen, and obedient to the laws of his country.

To which we may add, that, after the commission of crimes, there arise remorses and secret horrors, which give no rest to the mind, but make it have recourse to religious rites and ceremonies, as expiations of its offences. Whatever weakens or disorders the internal frame promotes the interests of superstition: And nothing is more destructive to them than a manly, steady virtue, which either preserves us from disastrous, melancholy accidents, or teaches us to bear them. During such calm sunshine of the mind, these spectres of false divinity never make their appearance. On the other hand, while we abandon ourselves to the natural undisciplined suggestions of our timid and anxious hearts, every kind of barbarity is ascribed to the supreme Being, from the terrors with which we are agitated; and every kind of caprice, from the methods which we embrace in order to appease him. *Barbarity, caprice*; these qualities, however nominally disguised, we may universally observe, form the ruling character of the deity in popular religions. Even priests, instead of correcting these depraved ideas of mankind, have often been found ready to foster and encourage them. The more tremendous the divinity is represented, the more tame and submissive do men become his ministers: And the more unaccountable the measures of acceptance required by him, the more necessary does it become to abandon our natural reason, and yield to their ghostly guidance and direction. Thus it may be allowed, that the artifices of men aggravate our natural infirmities and follies of this kind, but never originally beget them. Their root strikes deeper into the mind, and springs from the essential and universal properties of human nature.

[1] DIOD. SIC. lib. XX. 43.
[2] CIC. CATIL. i. 6, SALLUST. de bello CATIL. 22.

XV

GENERAL COROLLARY

Though the stupidity of men, barbarous and uninstructed, be so great, that they may not see a sovereign author in the more obvious works of nature, to which they are so much familiarized; yet it scarcely seems possible, that any one of good understanding should reject that idea, when once it is suggested to him. A purpose, an intention, a design is evident in every thing; and when our comprehension is so far enlarged as to contemplate the first rise of this visible system, we must adopt, with the strongest conviction, the idea of some intelligent cause or author. The uniform maxims, too, which prevail throughout the whole frame of the universe, naturally, if not necessarily, lead us to conceive this intelligence as single and undivided, where the prejudices of education oppose not so reasonable a theory. Even the contrarieties of nature, by discovering themselves every where, become proofs of some consistent plan, and establish one single purpose or intention, however inexplicable and incomprehensible.

Good and ill are universally intermingled and confounded; happiness and misery, wisdom and folly, virtue and vice. Nothing is pure and entirely of a piece. All advantages are attended with disadvantages. An universal compensation prevails in all conditions of being and existence. And it is not possible for us, by our most chimerical wishes, to form the idea of a station or situation altogether desirable. The draughts of life, according to the poet's fiction, are always mixed from the vessels on each hand of JUPITER: Or if any cup be presented altogether pure, it is drawn only, as the same poet tells us, from the left-handed vessel.

The more exquisite any good is, of which a small specimen is afforded us, the sharper is the evil, allied to it; and few exceptions are found to this uniform law of nature. The most sprightly wit borders on madness; the highest effusions of joy produce the deepest melancholy; the most ravishing pleasures are attended with the most cruel lassitude and disgust; the most flattering hopes make way for the severest disappointments. And, in general, no course of life has such safety (for happiness is not to be dreamed of) as the temperate and moderate, which maintains, as far as possible, a mediocrity, and a kind of insensibility, in every thing.

As the good, the great, the sublime, the ravishing are found eminently in the genuine principles of theism; it may be expected, from the analogy of nature, that the base, the absurd, the mean, the terrifying will be equally discovered in religious fictions and chimeras.

The universal propensity to believe in invisible, intelligent power, if not an original instinct, being at least a general attendant of human nature, may be considered as a kind of mark or stamp, which the divine workman has set upon his work; and nothing surely can more dignify mankind, than to be thus selected from all other parts of the creation, and to bear the image or impression of the universal Creator. But consult this image, as it appears in the popular religions of the world. How is the deity disfigured in our representations of him! How much is he degraded even below the character, which we should naturally, in common life, ascribe to a man of sense and virtue!

What a noble privilege is it of human reason to attain the knowledge of the supreme Being; and, from the visible works of nature, be enabled to infer so sublime a principle as its supreme Creator? But turn the reverse of the medal. Survey most nations and most ages. Examine the religious principles, which have, in fact, prevailed in the world. You will scarcely be persuaded, that they are any thing but sick men's dreams: Or perhaps will regard them more as the playsome whimsies of monkies in human shape, than the serious, positive, dogmatical asseverations of a being, who dignifies himself with the name of rational.

Hear the verbal protestations of all men: Nothing so certain as their religious tenets. Examine their lives: You will scarcely think that they repose the smallest confidence in them.

The greatest and truest zeal gives us no security against hypocrisy: The most open impiety is attended with a secret dread and compunction.

No theological absurdities so glaring that they have not, sometimes, been embraced by men of the greatest and most cultivated understanding. No religious precepts so rigorous that they have not been adopted by the most voluptuous and most abandoned of men.

Ignorance is the mother of Devotion: A maxim that is proverbial, and confirmed by general experience. Look out for a people, entirely destitute of religion: If you find them at all, be assured, that they are but a few degrees removed from brutes.

What so pure as some of the morals, included in some theological systems? What so corrupt as some of the practices, to which these systems give rise?

The comfortable views, exhibited by the belief of futurity, are ravishing and delightful. But how quickly vanish on the appearance of its terrors, which keep a more firm and durable possession of the human mind?

The whole is a riddle, an ænigma, an inexplicable mystery. Doubt, uncertainty, suspence of judgment appear the only result of our most accurate scrutiny, concerning this subject. But such is the frailty of human reason, and such the irresistible contagion of opinion, that even this deliberate doubt could scarcely be upheld; did we not enlarge our view, and opposing one species of superstition to another, set them a quarrelling; while we ourselves, during their fury and contention, happily make our escape into the calm, though obscure, regions of philosophy.